How to Get Over a Past Relationship Faster Than You Think

How to Get Over a Past Relationship Faster Than You Think 2 1/2 Hours to Freedom

Is breaking up hard to do, or accepting it?

Stewart Marshall Gulley

2004

TABLE OF CONTENTS

I would like to thank the many friends, relationships, politicians, leaders, enemies and relatives for inspiring me to write this book.

Now, let's get this party started!

INTRODUCTION

We must face the fact when a relationship is over. Through wisdom and all of the facts in front of you, it is time to go on. Hopefully after finishing this book you will see some light at the end of your tunnel. Thank God there's a light and not another hidden bomb. Although I will be using biblical scriptures to get my point across, do understand the psychiatrist does the same thing but doesn't give God the credit. **Trust me, there's nothing new under the sun**. So whomever you get your spiritual strength from you can replace the name of God if you choose. It's like stewardesses are now called flight attendants, but the work is the same.

This book takes approximately two and half-hours to read. It will definitely open that heart of yours that is so burdened down. It's not that the partner left that hurts; it's that you weren't prepared that's killing you. You put all of your eggs in one basket, and not only did they take the eggs, they took the basket too!

You have tried everything you could think of. You even thought you'd try God one time only and make Him a one-night stand, but the memory and the pain are still there. There are some who are in relationships and have been living together for years, but no one faces the fact that someone needs to leave. Yes, you might say that you are handling it, but that's on the surface. Let them start bringing someone over, and watch your heart jump and all the little petty things you start coming up with, and all of a sudden there's the big uncalled-for finale that may end with someone getting hurt more so than ever!

Admit that it's over and now what? It works the same in alcoholic programs. They can't get help being an alcoholic or drug addict unless they admit it. There is a twelve-step program for everything we do that hurts or harms us. Advice is only good if you use it.

You are now the teacher, and there's a big chalkboard in front of you that's vacant. It's up to you what you will write and teach the class, which is composed of the many little students with feelings sitting in your heart. With the help of God or your higher power and a relationship with Him—not a fly-by-night fix—I'm going to bring all that has been taken away back to you with peace, understanding, and joy. God doesn't mind you getting someone else, but this time He wants you to make sure He goes along on the date. You might as well speak it by faith and say: "Within two and a half hours I'm going to be on my way to freedom."

Is it possible to get over the man or woman who just dumped you in a hurry? Sure it is. So not to waste your time, let's get right to the point.

"Do not be unequally yoked" (2 Cor. 6:14). "Can two walk together unless they agreed?" (Amos 3:3). I hate to jump at you with two Bible scriptures, but it will work for you if you let it. Be not unequally yoked as it is quoted; the Bible questions why a righteous person should marry or be close friends with an unrighteous person. This is the same with the relationship that you are trying to get over.

Why are you trying to love someone that doesn't love you? Semi-scripturally speaking from Mark 8:36: What type of profit do you gain by winning the person back but losing your mind at the same time? If you admit it to yourself, then you might be able to be helped. First of all, you saw all of the signs coming, but you refused to believe them. So you called a friend and discussed it; they kept telling you the same thing: "Darling, if I were you I would leave him alone." You insisted that he or she would she change.

What you didn't realize was that you were the one that was about to change, and it wasn't going to be a pretty picture.

f

You were developing a habit of self-pity and hoping for something that would never materialize. It is like looking at a picture on the wall with a droopy flower, and you keep staring at it hop- ing it will change, but it doesn't. What you see is what you get. Better yet, what you see will eventually turn into what you are really going to get.

It is the same way as it is with drugs or alcohol. People have told friends to leave it alone, but instead they keep on until they are dependent and look like a sheepdog that has been washed in a washing machine. Then they seek rehabilitation where they have to overcome withdrawals; it's not easy, but you have to start somewhere.

You have to start right where you are to get over this per- son who has come to the conclusion that they don't want to be with you anymore, regardless of how many years you have spent together. There is a time and season for everything, and it just so happened to be your time—and definitely your unexpected season.

Realize within yourself that you hurt. Of course it does. It's that throbbing pain that makes you say, "Lord, just let me die." I can hear the Lord reply, "Die? What about me?" In other words, you have put your whole life into this individual and for- got about God. Don't you know that God is jealous? He doesn't mind you having a relationship, but don't put anybody before Him.

Relationships come and go. You miss one bus and another one comes along. Then you say to yourself, "But that bus was so nice. I put my whole world in it. Plus, we had children." Look! Those children will grow up and as soon as their flesh starts crawling, they won't see you at all because they will go seeking

for love themselves. Later to find out they were too soon old and too late smart.

Now that you've realized you are hurting, feeling lonely, and thinking that your whole world is about to end, imagine that you are $1 away from being totally broke. Now picture yourself going to the casino, putting that last dollar of hope into the slot machine, and hitting $10,000. Feeling a little better, huh?

This is what you have left: that little pinch of hope that can help you see that you are never alone; God is always there. He will get your attention once again. When something devastating happens to us, He is the first person we call on, and He is usually saying, "Oh, you finally decided to look me up? As the cell phone commercial goes, "CAN YOU HEAR ME NOW?"

KILL THAT FISH

With fifty percent of the marriages ending in divorce don't be embarrassed of yours. You're on the right side that faced reality and refused to continue to suffer in an unwanted relationship. Sad, but divorce is popular and the lawyers are getting rich. It's like a new face-cream that gets rid of wrinkles instantly.

We spend a lot of time trying to catch that big prize fish. We buy the best fishing pole, the best line, and the best bait. We even buy a new hat so we look presentable. Then we throw out the line. After much waiting and constant nibbling, we finally hook the fish. Little do we know, however, that the fish is full of problems.

We take the fish home, clean it, batter it, cook it, and eat it. All of a sudden, we begin to feel our stomachs swell to the point of throwing up; the fish was sick and now we are too.

We never know what we are getting in life, nor do we know why we change. We can surely put the shoe on the other foot. What if *you* were the one who left? It'd be okay then, right? How many people have you turned down without realizing that they went home and cried? Love hurts, and the wrong love at a very weak period in your life can almost kill you. Just remember the last dollar. There is still hope.

There are times in our lives that we have to go cold turkey, and sometimes that can be very rough. If a person leaves you, the first thing to do is accept it. All the crawling on the floor is only going to get you some bad calluses on your knees, leaving you with two problems. Why add to the misery?

Constantly calling them and asking them why is only going to cause aggravation and deepen the wound. You might as well pour alcohol in the cut and get the scream out now so we can deal with the healing process. A good approach is to stay away. How can you stop being an alcoholic if you're working at a liquor store?

If you take a fish out of the water and leave him out long enough, he will surely die. First of all, he's shocked that he got caught, same as it is in your relationship: Your partner is shocked that you are not constantly calling, when you were the one that was so madly in love.

The next stage for the fish is grasping for air. There you are breathing heavily, wanting to taste just a little more of that water, so you insist on seeing them one more time. You are still breathing heavily. You are looking at the water. You have taken out all the old pictures and started reminiscing about all the good old times. You're still looking at the water, but you must realize that water you are now looking at hasn't been filtered; it only looks pure. If you go back and get another taste, you will be sick again. Put away the pictures for now, and keep the fish out of the water and let it die.

The longer you stay away right now, the better you will feel. What the partner will do because of guilt is call you every now and then to see how you're doing. The best thing to do, however, is to politely tell them not to call you for a few weeks or even a month because you want to spend time alone. Or they don't have to call at all.

What has happened is that we have forgotten who we are. We were so used to that individual that we became addicted. When we were in the relationship, we should have spent time alone to deal with ourselves quietly and hear from God. You see, God was kind enough to allow us to love another human body, but He didn't mean for us to leave Him out. Now, since there's no one else around, we have to check in.

I can hear you saying now, "Lord, if you just help me get over this one, I promise you I won't get another one." Yes, right! As soon as this one is out of your system, here comes another one. Will you be wiser or very shrewd? What kind of bait will you use this time? True enough, there are many fish in the sea, but they all don't need to be in your boat. Realize that the older you get, the more you will find yourself alone, and you need to learn how to enjoy it.

In some relationships, people leave just because they are tired; others leave because they want someone younger; and then others leave because they were never there in the beginning, but they tried and hoped something would change. This is where many of us mess up. If the flame is not there, there is no need to try and build a fire. A person will click in your spirit, but you have to be honest: Do you really care?

It is so amazing how you can care and then all of a sudden not give a flip. What did that person do to turn you off? Believe me, it can happen. It can be as crazy as their bad breath.

TWO PEOPLE

There was a song that Patti Labelle used to sing years ago that said, "How is it that two people can laugh together, cry together, and one end up with a broken heart? Tell me how is it?"

No one knows what happens or why it happens. It can even be frustrating because you have to tell an individual that their "services are no longer needed." How cruel! Basically that is what we're saying. We have held out long enough. Face it: If the shoe were on the other foot, you would tell everyone in the community that you were ready to break up and that individual was the last one to be told. Believe me, he or she already knew; they just weren't talking about it.

When you have to make yourself stay in a relationship, you are hurting both people involved. The individual doesn't feel the love and affection, and you definitely don't if you're the one that is not in love.

We used to have a saying when we were kids that went like this: "Love is sweet, love is pure, love is something that the doctor can't cure." I am certain that he can't. The closest he can come to a cure is to give you a bunch of sleeping pills, and that's not a cure; it's just a little rest from worrying about what you refuse to accept.

You can talk to every person in the world about your dying relationship, but it will get to the point that they will hate to see you coming. Why? Because everyone knows that he or she is seeing someone else and isn't coming back anytime soon. Then again, they may not be seeing anyone. If they are happy, I'm sure that's a whole lot of peace.

Who knows? God may be preparing you for the right person, but you have put yourself through a few changes because of those hormones that got worked up and out of place. Now we have to work at getting them under control again. Can you imagine the withdrawal symptoms just from sex alone? You were having it constantly, and then all of a sudden there is none. Especially if it was good sex. Lord, have mercy! Kill that fish again!

HOW LONG WILL IT TAKE?

Now that's a good question. How long did it take for you to learn to ride a bike, or type, or even tie your shoe? It always depends on where the individual is mentally. The greatest thing that can happen is to grasp on to a strong spiritual commitment. Remember that although you feel alone, you are not.

It is an everyday struggle, and some get over partners faster than others, but if you don't find something to fill that void, it will take you much longer. Definitely try not to go to your favorite places you shared yet. There are so many nice places you were blinded by during the relationship that are equally nice. Who's to say that you need to go with someone? Try going alone. You can handle it. You were born alone and will die alone.

Sometimes getting over a person very fast can be shocking. You would probably say to yourself, "Gosh, I didn't know I could get over them that fast. I wonder if I loved them at all." Believe me, if you ever loved them in life, you still do, but it will be just a memory! Even years down the road, when you see that individual again, you'll start having flashbacks and goose pimples. The great thing about it though will be that you're not crying and hurting.

Sometimes breaking up is healthy for both parties. You can hinder one another in that personal freedom you want, as well as in career opportunities. When two individuals are into one another, there are not a lot of problems. Of course, there are some, and many times they are petty. If you come from a large family and marry or start dating a person that's an only child, you may witness a little selfishness because they are used to being given everything they want. There is no countdown to the exact second to how long it will take to get over a person. You will know when you're over them because you will stop counting the days. If anything you will be counting the hours it will be before your new date will come to pick you up. Of course this will be after you've been alone for a while and searched your inner spirit. If you start dating too early the new person who may be eventually great for you will end up being a pacifier. Once you are weaned from the pacifier then you are ready for a real peaceful meal from someone else.

I GAVE THEM MY BEST YEARS

How many times have we heard that? Little do you know there's a great possibility that your best years are about to start. You have an open mind, a few scars—none that can't be healed—and the whole world in front of you. You may have thought your former days were better than what you're going through now. Trials come to make you strong. You never know what goodness you are headed towards with wisdom, knowledge and compassion now. Do not say, "Why were the former days better than these?" For you do not inquire wisely concerning this. Wisdom is good with an inheritance and profitable to those who see the sun. For wisdom is a defense as money is a defense, but the excellence of knowledge is that wisdom gives life to those who have it (Eccl. 7:10-12).

You may know where you've been, but you don't know everywhere you're going. I heard a saying that went: "If you want to predict the future, create it." Well said, but we must except the detours.

That relationship was just a detour in your life, and the almighty God had to help you get around it. A detour is only a stop in the road leading you to another path to reach the same goal. You will have freedom again, and more than likely you'll fall in love again. Of course you'll be scared, but it's all part of the game they call life. Nothing's promised. No pain, no gain.

What are your so-called best years that you gave up? When you thought you were young and you could have gone to college, but you stayed at home and played house instead? Or are

9

you talking about the years when you could have gone touring around the world with some rich person, but you turned them down to be with someone who eventually dumped you? Be not deceived; rich people dump people every day too!

Most definitely as far as careers are concerned, sure we are to try to achieve things in life. We gain all the wealth, all the popularity that we think is love, until one day we find ourselves hurt with no one, and so we ask the question: "For what profit is it to a man if he gains the whole world, and loses his own soul?" (Matt. 16:26).

Your best years will be when you can draw yourself to God, when you can ask Jesus into your life to lead and guide you to all truths. Sure enough, we want earthly bodies to touch and caress us, but if they are hurting, abusing, and misleading us, why should we spend so much time with them? "The heart is deceitful, above all things, and desperately wicked; who can know it?" (Jer. 17:9).

You know within yourself that you have changed on individuals without knowing why. You thought you liked them but realized you really didn't. Sometimes you had other motives but wouldn't express them to anyone. Now you want to have a pity party because someone has left you.

When you think about it, you really don't have any years at all. You have one day at a time to enjoy in the best and most honest way you can. If it happens to turn into a year or many years, so be it.

"COME INTO MY PARLOR,"
SAID THE SPIDER TO THE FLY

Oh, how well do we remember that saying? Only if the fly enters the spider's web will he get caught, not realizing he is tangled up in everything but God.

Have you ever been in love with someone who mistreated and abused you? If so, it probably seemed as though you couldn't leave; you were caught in a web. You believed that it was more dangerous if you left. My, my, did the spider fool you! It made you so dependant that you believed you would have to start life all over again if you left. So, determining that you were just too old for that, you sat and suffered.

Many sit there and suffer until they die, not realizing that if they caught a grip that they could live again. Where is that trust in God? Has God failed you, or did you fail God—or do you even know whom I am talking about? Every step we take in life is a step of faith, regardless if things are going well or not. The spider can get you into its web and just leave you with all the responsibility and problems. In some cases it is a waste to the spider to even try to eat you for the feast because he feels he has done all of the damage he can.

So, let's look at it from that point of view. Here you are, this simple little fly caught up in a web, and you don't know what to do. Well, let's look at the web. It was built in squares, each one representing a step of your life. So instead of looking at the whole web wondering how you are going to get out of it, try taking one step at a time. Go around each square; look in one direction only, toward the edge of the web. Once you fall off the edge of anything, you then have to fly!

Every day is a step toward freedom once we realize we are tangled up in a web that didn't bring us freedom and happiness anyhow. The spider doesn't want you. It did at first and built an entire world around you, yet for some strange reason once it was built, you were left there. Whose fault was it?

Were you so blind that you were too busy receiving all of the fine things in life and not paying attention to the spider? Had you become so materialistic and demanding that the spider got tired and said, "I'm spinning my last web"? Did you add some little "spiderettes" to the family, only making your demands greater?

After all this, you tell your friends that, to your surprise, one day he or she came home and dumped you just like that. No, no, my friend. It was happening all along; they just finally made a decision to let it go.

Regardless if anyone is to blame, the decision that they finally came to is the same decision that you must come to. They are gone and the relationship is over.

Oh, but you're mad and want to get revenge because this person shouldn't be able to get away with that so easy. They messed up your heart and used you like an old dishrag. So you will make their life miserable by many harassing phone calls and letters, stopping by their house, and anything you can think of to make them miserable. Now guess what? After all of that, you still won't get them back. As a matter-of-fact, they'll probably be afraid of you. They might begin to hate you for your vengeance tactics. The less they are in contact with you, the better off they feel.

Children or no children involved, you have made them feel that they don't want to see you any more. If they were honest enough to tell you that it is over, why couldn't you be honest enough to accept it? I can hear you now: "You just don't know how this feels. I spent all of my time and money, and look what they did to me." WHY, YOU SELFISH LITTLE WHIMP! This person could have stayed and made your life miserable; at least you know it's over instead of wondering if it's going to be over. They were feeling miserable too.

Well, count your blessings. They could have shot you! You probably just said, "Well, I would have been better off." Yes, you would have, had you had Jesus in your life, but he's like an American Express credit card: Don't leave home without Him. In life, if you are taken out of here you want to make sure Jesus is on the inside.

We never know what is going to happen. We want to believe that we have the ideal person and relationship—but believe me, it is just an illusion. You will turn over one day and look at that individual that you have been toiling with for years and wonder, "Will I ever be able to collect the insurance money?" What cruel thinking that is; after all, you might go first.

We make everyone else miserable when we suffer when we don't have to. We take these bad marriages or relationships to our jobs and expect everyone to deal with us regardless of how we treat them. All we are having is a pity party, yet we're the only ones attending—and we don't even have enough sense to bring ourselves a gift. That gift is a sense of freedom and the love of God, who can only replace that which is taken. Remember all of the time you took to date that person. Try dating God for a while and see if He thinks about leaving you.

After you have your pity party, turn the lights out and go to bed; you've been up long enough dancing to the same record. It's a new world, so go get some CDs. (Christ Delivers).

I DIDN'T KNOW I WAS FREE

There was a little boy who had a jar of fleas. The top of this jar had little holes so that the fleas could breathe. As the boy watched the fleas in the jar, he noticed they kept jumping up and down to the top of the lid. After many weeks of this jumping, the fleas had been trained to jump to the top of the lid. After thinking about it, the little boy decided to open the jar and let the fleas go free. To his amazement, after he opened the jar, the fleas refused to jump past the edge of the jar; they had gotten used to only jumping to the top. Here they were, finally free, and would not go any further because they had been mentally trained in a little comfort zone!

This is how some of our lives are. The love of our life has decided to leave us and let us go free. We have become dependant and think that we cannot go any further in life without them. Here is the whole world now wanting us, but we will not go. It is all in the mind.

The only time we will accept a person leaving us is through death—and some refuse to believe that death is so final. If this person is still on earth breathing, however, we believe that they should be breathing beside us. The fact of the matter is that if we are not happy or that individual is not happy, we are sucking the breath out of one another; it's almost as if one gets asthma when the other is around.

The longer you wait to turn around, the longer you waste your time in an imaginary world, unless the almighty God intervenes. Every day that you wait to make up your mind is a day wasted. The individual that left you is on his or her way to peace and victory, yet here you are at home using boxes of tissues sobbing in your tears. The first box of tissue is okay, but when you go through cases and get to the point where you are borrowing tissues from your friends, you have a big problem. You have made a god out of something that is not God—nowhere near God; if they were, they wouldn't have left you.

The Bible tells us that what God has put together, let no man put asunder. The key words are "what God has put together." We go through this world half the time not knowing the difference between God and the Devil. There are times when we've said that God did it, when it could have been the Devil setting us up for the kill.

When you get to heaven, and I hope that you do, you will not think about that person who tried to take your joy from you here on earth. If they want to go, let them go. Every now and then, like the fleas in the jar, one just might get the nerve to go past the edge and realize it's not so bad out there after all. He will then try to go back and encourage the others to take a chance and try some new adventures.

Or the flea might say, "Let's go visit some of those fleas who have never been captured. They don't know what it is like to be bound down with problems and worries, wondering: When will that person be home? Who is he or she talking to on the phone? Whose number is that in his wallet? Why is he or she talking so softly?" This new group of fleas may not be insecure; they may know what they want.

The question again is: How long will they know what they want? Nothing is promised. You need to enjoy life while you can, hurt when you're supposed to, and go on when you have to. I would hate for you to be holding on to something only to end up with the matter getting worse. The next thing you'll be saying is "I should have let you stay out there when you were there."

Do you remember the story about the snake? A young man found a snake, and the snake charmed him and talked to him, so the young man brought the snake in the house. As time went on, the snake decided to show his true self and bit the young man. The snake told him, "Well, you knew I was a snake when you took me in."

There are some things we know, but we refuse to accept them. If a person feels they need to go, let them go. One of the very best and first signs is when they tell you they need a little space. Stevie Wonder can see that problem coming. It's really not a problem, however, because there are some people who do need space. What type of space are you speaking of? For business, you're writing a book, or are you just truthfully sick of being there?

God gives people different gifts and talents, as well as responsibilities. If you are hindering them from doing their work, the only answer for them is to get away. Usually, when a person tells us that God said a certain thing to him or her, we become hesitant about being very selfish, hoping God won't do something to us if we prevent a person from doing his or her work.

We must realize that love is very selfish. We want a person to feed our desires when and where we want them. When this love decides to leave us, we get all broken into pieces as though that was the "last person on earth."

Well, to those who can't get a grip, resorting to such foolish extremes as committing suicide, it *will* be "the last person they see on earth." If you kill yourself, you still don't have anybody, not even a chance to get healed or find anyone else. I wonder: Whom do you think you're going to meet? God or the Devil?

Suicide is committed by those who refuse to trust God and believe what the Devil tells them to do.

THE GRASS ISN'T GREENER
ON THE OTHER SIDE

True enough, the grass is not always greener on the other side. As a matter-of-fact, it's not grass; it's AstroTurf®. It's just an artificial look and a bunch of promises, a whole lot of maybes and somedays.

What if the grass was greener on the other side? What if it was real good grass in rich soil waiting for you, but you could not see it because you had built a liking for this artificial grass and couldn't let go?

There are some cases where a person isn't artificial, but there are some plants that don't grow well with certain grass. This person is everything you desired, and you were just all into them. You never really got the same response from them. Deep inside, this individual was wishing that you would stop caring so much because he or she isn't really sure where this relationship is going. You, however, start talking about doing things in the future, and they haven't made it through the day.

What puzzles me is how people can date for seven or eight years—or more—and not get married. I guess they don't want that official label put on their heads and that feeling of responsibility. If you're in a situation like that, you can walk away on any day and at any time with no strings attached.

If they are the only person in your life, I guess you are married in a sense, but I suppose you're not really sure if you want to be married to that one the way the world sees it. Some people make their own vows to one another without using the judicial system. Although marriage is not the issue here; the issue is that when one of you gets tired of the other, someone is going to be hurt.

A person can also be hurt because they want to leave a person. They sometimes think that they caused all of this pain, that it's their fault. It *is* their fault if they don't get out of the relationship that they don't want to be in! Hey! If you don't feel it, you just don't feel it.

Isn't it amazing how you can meet a person and think that they just walked out of a magazine, while someone else thinks the complete opposite? It's all in the mind. You never know how you're going to feel about a person or how long the feeling will last. Enjoy it while you can, but keep some tissues in your back pocket. They work just like auto insurance: You never know when there will be a major accident.

I'M LOOKING AT YOU ON PAPER

This may seem strange, but go get a piece of paper and write down all of the things that you liked about this person that left you. Now write down all of the negative things this person started doing. Take the "bad list" and throw it in the trash. Take the "good list" and burn it up. As you are burning it, just say to the list, "You were a good person, but you were just too hot for me."

Everything is an act of faith regardless of how we might look at it. How can a person who has a list of negative behaviors cause you to still be so attached after they've left you? They simply beat you to the punch. You already thought they weren't good for you; they just finally made it official.

The approval of any person comes from within your heart. If you are too blind to see that someone isn't into you, you will be making lists all of your life wondering who will you set on fire next.

How do you get rid of a mountain? One shovel at a time. It's a day-to-day thing, baby!

AFTER YOU'RE CAUGHT,
IT'S NEVER THE SAME

This person you love so much and can't seem to get over now has you thinking back to all you went through with them, but they still aren't staying. You're remembering the time you caught this person with someone else. It almost killed you, yet you stayed there to prove to them that you loved them—but they can't seem to see that, right? Better yet being caught is as bad as your first argument when you called each other bad names, your first physical fight or first slap. In which all of these will reveal the secret monster that lives within us. Knowing that the relationship takes on a whole different feeling after such a dramatic performance.

I know how you feel, and I can feel your heart, but just the mere fact that you caught them also brought a damper on the relationship. Once you catch a person in the act of cheating, there's a new countenance that comes about. Yes, you very well may have forgiven them, although you will never forget. You will hear this again, but a brother offended is harder to win than a strong city, and contentions are like the bars of a castle (Prov.18: 19).

You may have forgiven them, but they probably can't forgive themselves. If you stay in the relationship, every time they go out, they believe that you think they are doing something bad; sometimes they are, but sometimes they are not. Regardless, after some time these feelings of guilt, obligation, and constant looking over the shoulder wear on a person, leading them to the conclusion that it is best to get out of the relationship.

When this happens, you, of course, think that you two should hold on longer and maybe something positive will happen. Now, I don't have all of the answers, but unless some great spiritual miracle happens with God, it is best to let them go. If not, you will always be wondering what they're doing, and they will be always be wondering what you *think* they are doing—and the cheating will surely be brought up in argument after argument, even long after the fact. Eventually through aggravation they may be forced to cheat again.

When they come to the conclusion that the best decision is to separate, this individual is probably doing you both a big favor. Someone has to come to the conclusion that one of you must be strong and say that it is time to call it off.

A person that gets caught in the act can become very angry and hostile—because you caught them, of course. They often act this way because of internal guilt and feelings of lowliness; however, whether you followed them or came home early, caught is caught! Being caught is not any fun. I've gotten caught before and I thought it was the worst day of my life. Dying at that moment would have felt so much better.

Regardless of how much time you have spent with one another, if a person decides they have to go, you must respect their decision. Why torture each other? If you're not happy and there are children in the picture, they won't be able to see happiness either.

Only through prayer and faith can any of these things change. It is just like accepting Jesus: We all have a free will. Deep down in your heart, you cannot make up a love for an individual; if the feeling is not there, it's just not there. There are some cases we don't believe anything. We'd have to be like the story in Mark 9:24 where the man had a deaf and dumb child and he asked Jesus to help his unbelief.

How many times have we heard the line, "Oh, I'll always love you and want you as a friend"? At this point who wants to hear that friend crap? They probably will want you as a friend, but if you want them to love you more, it's best you let them go; otherwise, it will turn into a nagging situation. It will get to the point where when you pull up in the driveway, he or she will be inside saying, "Oh, God, here comes that butthole."

Have you heard the saying "Absence makes the heart grow fonder"? It sure does, especially when you don't want to be there. The heart would really like to be free. Can you imagine the pressure and stress on your arteries, just because you don't want to let go? Stress is a silent killer. Many have died dating it.

Think about how you felt before you met this individual. You may have been a little lonely, but you were probably happy and didn't have a lot of bad feelings. You have to take your mind back to that point and replace that void. Only you can do it.

It's like someone stealing your floor-model television. Every time you come home, you have to look at that empty space. One day, however, you'll either have to get another one or you'll have to decide to change the furniture around to make things look presentable, especially if you can't afford a new one.

That's how we have to handle our hearts: We have to change the feeling around inside and replace that void. The more we concentrate on that void, the bigger the problem appears, even though it is still the same size. No more, no less, the fact is that you are still hurt and feeling rejected. Once again, I turn it back on you: What if you were the one that decided to break it off? Oh, yeah, it's still all right if it's in your favor!

Think about it this way: If your house catches on fire, of course you will be very devastated; however, if you had fire insurance, you know you can replace all but the memories.

The only insurance we have in life is the love for Jesus

Christ, and this can only be felt or built up if you spend some time with Him. You physically can't stay in the Bible all day and night and run to church and go haywire; you have to do things with discretion. There's a time and place for everything. Practicing the word of God a little bit every day will take you far. It's similar to the slogan from Bit-O-Honey® candies: "A little bit—o-honey goes a long, long way."

Here you are, sitting in a corner and thinking you're about to die because you caught him or her in the bed with one of your relatives or best friend. What a slammer! You don't know it yet, but all it did was release you and help you to understand what was around you. What's done in the dark will come to the light.

If you still choose to suffer and deal with it once it has come into light, then don't blame anyone but yourself. That person is going to carry on with only a small amount of guilt on their shoulder, while you're about to take a knife and cut your heart out. Now there's more pain. Put the knife away, or go cut up a head of lettuce.

I caught a girlfriend one time hugging one of my customers at her apartment. I had driven by her house and was looking at her second-floor apartment window. I almost flipped. When I knocked, the man took off through the back door, so I ran after him—that's when I discovered it was a customer of mine. I told him, "I just wanted to see who you were." It almost killed me.

I told God, "If you take this feeling out of my heart, I will never fall in love again." I know you've said that before, too. Of course, I fell in love again, and guess what? I caught her cheating too. That time, however, the feeling was different; I just went on about my business.

That's the breaks in life. Unfortunately, I've even been the one to be caught too. When it happens, you want to blow your own brains out. To God be the glory! Thank God for second chances—because it's not a pretty sight.

Maybe the next time you sneak to follow someone it will be to the house of God where they are getting filled with the Holy Ghost. Now that's what you call getting caught with a good ending. It's not that you are not saved if you don't, but it's the extra power you need. In other words you've been running your car on regular gas, but you didn't know you needed premium.

The reason I speak of this is because it is so played down in many churches and is desperately needed all over the world. If you really want to change your world seek the Holy Ghost. As Jesus said in the bible, if it were not so I would have told you! What are you afraid of? You ask for everything else. Luke 11: 11-13 reads: If a son asks for bread from any father among you, will he give him a stone? Or if he asks for a fish, will he give him a serpent instead of a fish? Or if he asks for an egg, will he offer him a scorpion? If you then, being evil, know how to give good gifts to your children how much more will your heavenly Father give the Holy Spirit to those who ask Him!"

YOU'RE WALKING ALONE

Whether you know it or not, you are walking by yourself with no direction. If you would ask for wisdom, you would find a new partner. At this point, however, the only one that is available is God.

"How can two walk together unless agreed?" (Amos 3:3). If the love of your life asks you to go to the store with him or her and you agree, then it is quite evident that you will get to the store without one pulling against another. If someone tries to make you go when you don't want to; it's like pulling a stubborn mule. By you agreeing, the trip to the store can be quite pleasurable.

This scenario is similar to what can happen when someone tries to force someone to stay in a relationship. The person tries everything to get this mule to come to his or her side but winds up talking about the mule, cursing it out, calling it bad names, and badmouthing it to friends.

The next thing they know, the mule is asleep and hasn't heard a word that's been said. The mule knows that the same thing is going to be repeated every day in an attempt to make him feel guilty as to why he is not budging. Eventually, he will walk out of the door to freedom. He may have a few bruises from being kicked around, but what the heck, he's free.

You see, in a relationship that's being pulled apart, first you hear all of the excuses about how they get on each other's nerves. Then they're staying away from each other more often, leading to more fussing and complaining. It's just like a pimple: One day it will come to a head, and "pop goes the weasel"; everything explodes, leaving you with one big mess on your hands.

Being real with ourselves can be very hard, but that's the only thing that works. If the person doesn't want to be there, you must realize that they are not in agreement with the relationship anymore and that you are walking alone.

Complaining, feeling that God has forsaken you, and all of this crap doesn't make any sense—especially when you thought this relationship was for life because you had "so much in common." What you didn't have in common was that you were in it *for* life, and they were in it *because of* life.

Life draws us to someone or someone to us, for however long, we never know. When you are in the state of walking alone again, you understand that there is only one thing promised to you: the love of God. We are running around here putting all of our trust in others, when there is only one person that will be true to us in return. "Let God be true, but every man a liar" (Rom. 3:4).

Although we try to be the perfect one, obstacles will still come in our way. Putting up a front while you are hurting inside is not healthy for anyone. I thought I had the perfect marriage. We both had hair salons, nice clothes, and the whole works. We didn't get married because of love but because of sin; she became pregnant. I thought the best thing to do was to marry her because if I hadn't, she told me she was going to have an abortion, which was something that I didn't want to happen.

We went through with the marriage, and I was miserable until I came to grips with the fact that although she was nice, she wasn't for me. She cared for me, but I knew she wasn't in love with me. She became very bitter because of my decision and rebelled against me. I just wanted to be free and happy. Giving her the house, Mercedes, and most of my furniture was not enough;

she got our daughter too, whom I wanted. All I got was a bunch of name-calling and child-support letters.

I did most of the cooking, coordinating and designing the inside our home, and decision-making, although my actions were not out of love. We had a housekeeper and a baby-sitter and shared all the expenses, which balanced out, but I wasn't happy. I asked God for forgiveness, and I went on with my life. I remarried, and so did she.

Ironically she's not with the person she married nor am I. As a special warning, be careful when people are always telling you that the two of you look good together. It's a possibility you'll look good beside anyone you stand with. The power of suggestion can get you messed up sometimes. People will put you together and when problems arise they are no where around.

I could have remained there had I not wanted to be honest with myself. There are people who stay in relationships for years and years even though they are miserable. Some get to the point that they have several jobs just to avoid going home. Others get involved with many activities that don't include the spouse; they will trim all around the bush instead of clearly seeing that it needs to be cut down.

I heard of a case where a husband and wife could not deal with one another, so they finally filed for a divorce. After the divorce was final, they started messing around with one another sexually. When they'd been married, nothing happened because he had another girlfriend—which the wife found out about, but the husband insisted on seeing her. I guess he had the "couldn't help its."

I'm sure I could write several books about the different types of unhappy relationships where no one wants to step up to the plate and hit the truth-telling homerun. Perhaps they don't want to see "THIS IS NOT WORKING" lit up in the scoreboard.

Walking alone works well, until you bump into the person that dumped you. So try walking down another street; there are a lot of pretty neighborhoods out there. The shrubbery you were looking at had some bad roots—but thank God for root killer. Now you can live again.

LETTING GO WITH MAGNETS

Here you are trying your best to let go of this person—even after they told you that they needed space or that the relationship was over—but you still want to call them or see them one more time. Hate to bust your bubble, but realize he or she has become a magnet and is trying to pull you in. It's not going to work.

Their magnet is drawing them to something else; it can just be freedom, not necessarily another person. Your magnet is holding on with all of its might, wasting all of your "what's-left energy" trying to pull this person back.

My friend, deal with the pain and ask what Regis Philbin would: "Is this your final answer?" Accept it; the person wants to leave. The best thing you can do is to help them. If you are living together and therefore it would be too disturbing for you to be there when he or she moves out, make sure you're not home when they do so.

Sometimes you have to let go. Who knows? They might decide that they want to come back—if you let them. Of course, some of us will say, "If you walk out of that door, you can never come back." Sure, that's what you're saying, but if they walked back in that door we'd probably jump all over them. The risk in that is how many times can a person walk out of the door, leaving and hurting you each time?

What if you decided that if they walk out that they could truly not come back? Do you think they would think twice about returning? If they are not really in love with you or concerned about you, they had better not return, because they are going to catch pure hell. You just might throw them out next time if it seems they are going to act up just a little bit.

Make up your mind and go ahead and live your life. Don't be like Lot's wife in the Bible and look back and turn into a pillar of salt. If the past has done nothing else but hurt you why are you looking back as though you want to visit the pain? You're at a point in your life that you should turn your magnet over and not worry about pulling in anything but the love of God. He's always willing to draw!

Don't worry about all of the money you threw away on the person because if you keep your sanity, you can make much of it back and possibly more. You will find out that the amount of money you thought you needed in the relationship is not what you needed at all. You simply had a high budget for them, and they were simply enjoying the luxury, whether it was selfishness or a sense of guilt because they didn't know how to tell you not to waste your money—because you weren't going to be around very long.

A magnet can be a dangerous force especially if it is built with negativity. I talked to a person one time who told me that his girlfriend had been using him for the past five years. I chuckled and told him that she can use him five more if he wanted her too. Waking up can be a beautiful thing!

Wake up and be in love again, but start with yourself. God introduced you to yourself, now thank Him for what He's teaching you.

GIVE ME LIBERTY OR GIVE ME DEATH

Wouldn't it be nice if there were a natural pill that would end the pain and return you to happiness and freedom again? Maybe there will be in the near future, but it's not available right now (a good joke huh?). Instead, people are using crutches such as drugs and alcohol, but they wind up being that much more miserable. Some even wind up dead.

You can be freed. There is no person worth you killing yourself over. Think about it: You kill yourself, you lose the chance to enjoy peace and the love of God, and the person you were so crazy over is out enjoying himself or herself. It just isn't worth it. Especially if married, think of all you have labored for to leave behind to a person who didn't have you in their heart any longer. As Eccl. 2:18 reads: Then I hated all my labor in which I had toiled under the sun, because I must leave it to the man who will come after me, and who knows whether he will be wise or a fool? Yet he will rule over all my labor in which I toiled and in which I have shown myself wise under the sun. This also is vanity.

I know you just want to die, but be happy that the truth came out and the relationship is over. "The end of a thing is better than its beginning. The patient in spirit is better than the proud in spirit" (Eccles. 7:8). Did you just read that? (I repeat) It said that the end of a thing is better than its beginning. Start looking for the better in your life.

Won't you be happy and full of joy when this terrible feeling ends? Through the love of Jesus Christ it will eventually happen. Some people get over breakups faster than others, and some try to hold on for life, but God because of His goodness, still knows how to get through to those too.

The mind that you have now is not beneficial to you or to God. He is waiting on you to begin to steer your mind in the right direction. "Do not conform to this world: but be transformed by the renewing of your mind, that you may prove what is that good and acceptable and perfect will of God" (Rom. 12: 2).

Transforming your mind as though you are saying "Garbage in, garbage out." Any individual that is causing you to hurt, suffer, and worry is not meant for you. That is a god that you need to let go. Until you realize it and make up your mind, your real God who is in heaven can't do a thing. Just like you asked for that man or woman who almost drove you crazy, you can ask that same God to set you free. Remember "Freedom" is not free. Someone has to pay the price to get it back. Also think of Jesus on the cross.

There are many gods, however I'm reminded of another story: There was a man in the desert worshipping a little statue he had carved from a piece of wood. A tourist was passing through the desert and stopped and asked him what was he doing. The man stated he was worshipping this god which was carved from a tree. The tourist began to look in the heavens and tears began to roll down his face and he nicely said, "You know that piece of wood you're looking at was made by my God, and I wouldn't have a God that I couldn't feel.

PEOPLE DON'T WANT TO BELIEVE IT,
BUT IT STILL WORKS

How is it that people talk about the Bible every day, yet it seems as though nothing is going right? Well, my friend, it's like this: Good advice is only good if you use it.

We have heard so much, and there are thousands of scriptures, but until we feed on it and ask God to help our unbelief, we will be sitting like knots on logs every day. Receiving the power of the Holy Ghost was one of the greatest miracles I had ever received. It serves as the additional flow of power we need to help us endure the obstacles of life, whether bad relationships, demanding jobs, prejudice, or any other negative problems. Rest assured troubles will come. Sorry to tell you, but you stepped into eternity the day you were born. Inside eternity situations do come.

You will realize this world is not worth a "hoot" and that you can't wait to get the "hell" out of here. I mean that literally! You can read about my experience of receiving this power in my book *If You Thought Columbine Was Something, You Haven't Seen Anything Yet*; which mostly deals severely with our youth.

As much as people are against it, they still run around and carry the same Bible, but they delete what they want. I'm not into denominations, but if you want to find out about receiving the power of the Holy Ghost, attend an Apostolic or Pentecostal church. I am not saying that you have to stay there forever. Just hang around for a spell and you just might catch on fire. Boy! They will wear you down. I went, and I'm glad I did. You still can be a Baptist, Methodist or whatever you decide. Just get that

Holy Ghost down in you and it will blow your mind as well as lead you. Can you imagine a person breaking up in a distressful relationship and get filled with the Holy Ghost? They haven't felt real love until that happens. There are other denominations that believe in it, but it's only a few where you can recognize or feel the presence of the Holy Ghost in full bloom. Don't be misunderstood by the denomination itself. Believe me the Pentecostal's go through all of the sins and problems as the other denominations. However, there is a stronger conviction and spiritual closeness. Yet they must be careful because some become haughty because of the gift they've received from the Lord in spite of their previous unrighteousness forgetting who they once were. It's almost like having a homeless person to become wealthy and now he holds his nose up in the air while gazing at the other homeless lying in the streets.

Do not be misled. All will not speak in tongues. If it is your desire, this you should ask of God. You may be an unbeliever in this area, however if you ask God he will help your unbelief.

We all have different gifts, but being filled with the Holy Ghost is a beautiful experience. You are filled with a language that you were never taught. Now I understand what it really means to be bilingual.

Back to speaking of sin, the word sin itself will cause your insides to jump because it is real and we hate to hear the word. Sin is in us all, but we must continue to ask God to help us. Listen to what Paul says in Romans 7:14-25: For we know that the law is spiritual, but I am carnal, sold under sin. For what I am doing, I do not understand. For what I will to do, that I do not practice; but what I hate, that I do. If then, I do what I will not to do, I agree with the law that it is good. Now, it is no longer I who do it, but sin that dwells in me. For I know that in me (that is, in my flesh) nothing good dwells; for to will is present with me, but how to perform what is good I do not find. **For the good that I will to do, I do not do, but the evil I will not to do, that I practice.** Now if I do what I will not to do, it is no longer I who do it, but sin that dwells in me. I find then a law, that evil is present with me, the one who will to do good. For I delight in the law of God according to the inward man. I see another law in my members, warring against the law of my mind, and bringing me into captivity to the law of sin which is in my members. O wretched man that I am! Who will deliver me from this body of death? I thank God—through Jesus Christ our Lord! So then with the mind I myself serve the law of God, but with the flesh the law of sin. (Also read Romans Chpt. 8).

We must understand that the law serves its purpose and Jesus came to fulfill the law because we couldn't do it. Therefore because he could, He is constantly helping us. Thinking of our everyday task. Can you imagine if there was no law to obey the traffic lights and we drove the way we wanted? Look at the damage it causes when those who choose not to obey.

Allow me to interject a few views about attending church through understanding of why it has become a turn off to many. The church of Jesus Christ has been held up so high that it is the most talked about religion there is. So obviously the problems that occur in it will always stand out. Not to exclude there are problems in all faiths. This goes from Chanting to the hail Marys. Anywhere any type of good is trying to be nurtured be assured that the Devil shows up. As in Job Chapter 2:1 reads: Again there was a day when the sons of God came to present themselves before the Lord and Satan came also among them to present himself before the Lord.

They were going to church. Satan always shows up. If he can discourage people from accepting and knowing Jesus he realizes that he doesn't have to show up there that often because they are already on the other side of the fence. Today we have this New Age group and other organizations speaking of these inner powers and the universe. Yes there is an universe, but we must give honor where honor is due (Rom.13:7) How would you like to do something fantastic and no one gives you credit as though they did the project? The crystals and the beads that some beliefs use, GOD MADE THEM. There is nothing wrong with it, they just need to know and accept that God is the creator. The earth is the Lord's and all of its fullness (Ps.24: 1). All things were made through Him, and without Him nothing was made that was made (John 1:3). I heard a comical story once of a man who had a quarrel with God stating that he didn't need God for anything. The man stated he would grow his own trees, plant his own vegetables, build his own houses and make anything he wanted. God said, "Fine, you just use your own dirt and water." How's that for logic?

WARNING: To those who don't believe the truth of God, He will send you a strong delusion that you should believe a lie instead of the truth. (2Thess.2:11). Does your denomination believe the truth of God? Do they believe in Jesus Christ? Your denomination may have good morals, in which all of them do. However the dangerous part of a lie is that some of it is true. Always enough to get you to believe different. Not acknowledging God for who he really is. There are some meetings that you may come upon that have good morals, positive enforcement but does not recognize any leader. For those who know Christ their information is good because, it gives them another fulfillment for the void they were feeling. As when they went to the traditional churches there was a lot of financial obligations mixed with the many services. A semi-scenario of this could be having a math teacher that teaches you how to count. Although he may not mention God or Jesus Christ you thank God for what he's taught you through the teacher.

There are many gangs in the world looked upon causiously because of the negativity they present.

However the church has constructed just as many gangs. The Baptist are against the Methodist and the Pentecostals are against the Science of Mind and they all are against each other because they are not of the same gang. Don't you think Satan is happy?

To top church off they have inner-gangs within each other. In other words some Baptist churches don't fool with the other Baptist churches. Such is the same in the rest of the denominations. Yes, the band played on as they all carry the same King James Bibles which is just one of the over 1600 versions of the Bible.

With all of this going on a person who has high hopes of going to church run into all of the jealousy and confusion while getting discouraged and not wanting to attend at all. Those who are strong must hold out because faith comes from hearing the word of God. Although you hear me speak of God, Jesus and the Holy Ghost I am referring to one. All three are wrapped up in God. To give you a quick example of this: Your name could be Susan. You are a mother, a secretary and a wife. You hold all three positions but when you are called you answer by the name of Susan. Of course the other three positions come with you. So is the same as calling on the name of Jesus.

Everything is wrapped up in His name. Whatever you do in word or deed, do all in the name of the Lord Jesus, giving thanks to God the Father through Him (Col.3:17). Now let's get back to discussing the five-fold ministry.

God has set the five-fold ministry in the churches: "He Himself gave some to be apostles: and some prophets; some evangelists; and some pastors and teachers for the equipping of the saints for the work of the ministry, for the edifying of the body of Christ" (Eph. 4:11).

The reason many of us are so frustrated and bent out of shape when relationships fail is because we are not fulfilled spiritually. When we are empty on the inside, the Devil can throw any negative bomb he wants on us because he knows the word of God isn't there to sustain us. Trust me, Satan knows the word of God. There's nothing like an educated fool.

Once you are filled with the Holy Ghost, should you decide to go that route; even if you don't, you still need to hear evangelists, apostles, preachers, teachers, and pastors. The average church only has a pastor, and he won't let evangelists or prophets come to help his members; therefore, the church becomes filled with weak members who will crack at any moment.

Can you imagine the person who has been to church for years and commits suicide because of a relationship that went bad? Where was the power on the inside, the word of God that was given from any of the positions in the five-fold ministry? My book "Why Churches Are Weak" explains much of this.

I believe that when the five-fold ministry is known, you must take this approach: Handle it as you did when you were getting ready to go out on a special date. You got your shoes from one store, your pants from another, your shirt from another, and so on. If the ministries won't bring it to you, it's best you go get it. "Seek and ye shall find, knock and the door will be open" (Matt. 7:7).

People will say that you are church hopping. Well, thank God I hopped around because I would have been in bad condition had I stayed at some of these churches. People are so afraid when you start talking about God because deep down they know He exists, regardless of whether or not they pay Him any attention. It's like a minister preaching over the pulpit. You know when he is punching your card and he doesn't know you are feeling guilty. However, you know the real truth inside.

Trust me. I know that a lot of people need help, but the rich folk are really in a world of trouble. Many don't believe or even think about God. I'm sure there are a few, but I don't know too many, if any, that are filled with the precious Holy Ghost and trying to do His will. Although many ministers have become filthy rich using the word of God it is a different subject due to how some of it has been done which is discussed in my book, "Why Churches Are Weak." If He allowed the rich to become rich, he can surely allow them to become poor. As Revelation 3: 17 reads: "Because you say, I am rich, have become wealthy, and have need of nothing—and do not know that you are wretched, miserable, poor, blind and naked. Some of our wealthiest people don't know that they still need Jesus. Understand this: 1Timothy 6:7- For we have brought nothing into this world, and it is certain we can carry nothing out. John 15:5- I am the vine, you are the branches. He who abides in Me, and I in him, bears much fruit; **for without Me you can do nothing.**

If you have just a little hope of God in you, live off of it, regardless of what you're going through. You will find God very challenging, especially when he starts taking you from glory to glory. Your neighbors can be shooting guns but you'll be in your house shouting and praising God because you have finally faced that the time is almost near and what this world is really about.

Have you ever had a dried plant with just one little green leaf on it? One day you decide to water it and eventually the whole plant comes alive after continuous nurturing. There is hope in everything God makes.

People may not want to believe, and often they shy away from the Bible. It really works, but you won't learn it all in a day.

It is almost magical how He reveals His word to you. One year you get a revelation about a scripture, and the next year He'll give you a new revelation about the same scripture.

Hang in there. God won't tell you that it's time we separate. If anything He's trying to tell you that He wants to get closer.

You don't know where you might be when someone will share the sincere word of God. Most of the times it will be a one on one experience and not in some large church, where their concentration is on building funds and camp meetings. You may be at a party, on the beach or in a nightclub. You have met many people who know Christ, but once you get into a one to one conversation you will realize of how much of God they know. He's everywhere and He knows just the right person to talk to you. He's that kind of God. . Here's what Paul said in the bible ICor.9:I9—For though I am free from all men. I have made myself a servant to all that I might win the more. To the Jews I became as a Jew that I might win Jews; to those who are under the law, as under the law that I might win those who are under the law; to those who are without law, as without law (not being without law toward God, but under law toward Christ). That I might win those who are without law; to the weak I became as weak that I might win the weak. **I have become all things to all men, that I might by all means save some.** Now this I do for the gospel's sake, that I may be partaker of it with you. As you notice his statements that **HE BECAME "AS." In other words he talked to people at their level because he had gone through some of the same things.**

Don't get so almighty and puffed up and judge one another regardless of where you meet them and how. Therefore let him who thinks he stands take heed lest he fall (ICor.I0:I2).

God is with us all the time but when we really seek Him he has to reveal Himself. Then we realize He was always there.

Think about this: Let's say you finally ran into your brother after many years and he kept telling you that he was a millionaire. You with plenty of doubt say, "Sure you are." The reason you feel this doubt because your brother doesn't live lavishly. One day after a few years he decides to take you to his bank. You hear the teller saying to him that he has a two million- dollar balance and you're able to see it on the computer. Now that you've seen it, you began to hold your head up and feel confident that if you needed anything he would be able to supply it.

That's almost how it is with Jesus. Once you really find out who He is you will have a different feeling about life.

IT'S TOO LATE TO POINT THE FINGER

In the Garden of Eden, the serpent convinced Eve to eat the fruit, some of which she gave to Adam. After this great act, God came along in the cool of the day asking, "Where art thou?" Of course, Eve blamed the serpent and Adam blamed Eve. At this point, however, it was too late to point the finger because they both ate the fruit and all three had to suffer the consequences—and so did we!

You can blame the other party, but regardless of your situation, both of you are the reason for the end result. Just because the person wanted something from you didn't mean you had to give it. Meanwhile, through all of your pain and suffering, neither of you are concentrating on the gifts God gave you. You are both so busy fighting negative energy that there are no positive results. When one person said, "No more," he or she really didn't mean it, so they fought with it a few more years. Time continued to pass with the same problems and same results.

God gave you both great talents and gifts, but you couldn't concentrate because you couldn't come to grips to get out of the relationship. Either you wouldn't let *them* go or they wouldn't let *you* go. Someone has to be man or woman enough to say, "No more," even if you're the one who's in love and therefore loses out temporarily.

You have to face it and free your mind. I can see it now: You're facing God and he asks you what did you do most of your life. You reply, "God, I would have been a preacher or a teacher like you told me to, but that woman you gave me gave me pure hell." God responds by saying, "Did you mention hell? I don't think you know what pure hell is yet, but maybe I should direct you there."

That would be a devastating moment for anyone. We want to put the blame for what God has called us to do on someone else. Just because the serpent speaks doesn't mean you have to answer. The Devil, that old serpent Lucifer, will try to discourage you and bring negativity into your life so that you will not be a blessing or means of encouragement to anyone.

What better prospect could he use besides your flesh and mind? He'll get you completely involved and tied up with someone that doesn't mean you any good; he'll even make you believe that you can't live without them; and once he gets you exactly where he wants you, he throws the knockout. That is when you feel your world has ended, when you feel like real trash. Well, good! One man's trash is another man's treasure.

You can be someone's treasure once you catch a hold of life and search for what God has intended you to do. Tapping into your gifts and desires is very important; it can bring you out of the misery you're in.

There are times in a relationship when the other partner will try to discourage you from doing what you need to do or what God has put in your heart. The result is that you have two people not doing what gift God has called them to do; plus, they can't get along with one another. What a frustrated house!

Did you ever see someone doing the very thing that was in your heart, but you just didn't have the vigor to try it because of a relationship that was pulling you down? You cannot treat a relationship as more important than God. When it's time for you both to face God, I'm sure your partner is going be thinking about what he or she is going to tell God, not about you.

Reach down inside yourself and pull out that positive thing

that means so much to you. You might say, "Well, if I do that, it's going to take eight years." If it's in your heart, God can make those eight years go by very swiftly. What can be more devastating when eight years have come and you hadn't done anything? Better yet, he can make a miracle happen without you stepping foot into a school just for your sincere effort. Never underestimate God when you step out on faith.

Why call on Him if you don't expect Him to answer? He has His ways of answering us all. The only way that we will receive joy is by using the main gift God has given us. He has given me many gifts, and I mean a load. I'm an auctioneer, artist, calligrapher, cosmetologist instructor, actor, author, playwright, clothing designer, choral director, cook, model instructor, and dancer. Most people can't believe it until they see me in motion. Half the time I can't believe it myself. I will try my fullest to do them all, but not at one time of course.

Guess what? None of them have fully prospered. Why? Because God told me to speak His word and motivate, so that's what I do! He didn't ask me about being perfect. He knew I wasn't worth a nickel when He called me. In the same breath He told me that I would be different and not of the norm. Believe me how truer said. If you consider yourself a child of God you are a minister in some form. One of Webster's definitions of minister is to aid or service. Roman 12:6—Having then gifts differing according to the grace that is given to us. Let us use them; if prophecy, let us prophesy in proportion to our faith; or ministry let us wait on our ministering: or he that teaches on teaching, he who exhorts, in exhortation; he who gives, with liberality; he who leads, with diligence; he who shows mercy, with cheerfulness. Let love be without hypocrisy. Abhor what is evil. Cling to what is good.

Don't let anyone blur your vision. God tells us clearly, but we won't believe its God until something drastic happens. It's like watching television. If you don't like what you see change the channel. Follow the very thing that you think about or continuously feel. When you get there, you'll definitely know it is God.

"Therefore we also, since we are surrounded by so great a cloud of witnesses, let us lay aside every weight, and the sin which so easily ensnares us, and let us run with endurance the race that is set before us" (Heb.12:1). As much as we don't want to, we must lay aside every weight and sin that is setting us back. Weight is just what it says. It will slow you down whether it is physically or mentally. If our minds are burdened down thinking and worrying about our relationship, we cannot progress. Not only will it hold you back for months, it will also still leave you hanging in remorse. *Let it go and run for your life!*

A story once told: In Africa every morning a Gazelle awakens knowing it must outrun the fastest Lion if it wants to stay alive…

Every morning a Lion wakes up knowing that it must run faster than the slowest Gazelle or it will starve to death…

It makes no difference whether you're a Lion or a Gazelle…

when the sun comes up you better start running.

Right before you met this person, you were probably seeking God, or you were very progressive. Then, all of a sudden, this person caught your eye, and slowly you started doing other things. You stopped going to meetings or to class, living it up, and not realizing what was taking place in your life. Once you fell head over heels, the so-called love of your life decided to go in another direction, and it tore your world down.

You were running so well. "Who did hinder you that you should not obey the truth?" (Gal. 5:7). Paul wrote this scripture to the Galatians, who believed in God but man came along and tried to turn them from the truth. This is the same with any of us. We know the truth. God has put the Ten Commandments in our hearts and we know when something doesn't feel right. This feeling is there whether we know a lot of scriptures or not. If certain things weren't wrong we wouldn't try to sneak and do them. We allow others to completely remove us from what our hearts desire.

There's another side to this, too. Some of us stay with people who give us a hard time about working on our careers, yet when we become successful, there they are trying to reap the benefits. If you don't stand your ground, you will be standing under someone else's feet.

You will have to fight for anything that you desire in life, and you'll have to fight to keep it, too. The Devil might be mad because you persevered, so make him mad by staying there and helping others to get there. Get the spirit of Harriet Tubman and the Underground Railroad, but don't lose your focus. Not everyone on the train is willing to stay aboard for the entire trip!

A friend of mine used to say, "If you look long, you look wrong." Sometimes what we keep looking at will try to destroy our whole life. If a person can't understand or is bothered by what you're doing, you really need to give them a rain check or tell them exactly what you're going to be doing and when you're going to do it. If they can't understand it and you therefore stop what you're doing, you will be asking yourself down the road, "What hindered me? I was doing so well at first."

"You ran well; who hindered you from obeying the truth?" This persuasion does not come from Him who calls you. A little leaven leavens the whole lump" (Gal. 5:9). In other words: One bad apple will spoil the whole bunch. Same as saying: Do not be deceived, evil company corrupts good habits (ICor.15:33). Are you getting the picture yet?

THANK GOD I LET GO

We never know how God is working in our favor until we look back at the results we could have received had we not let that person go. God sees the whole picture even before we begin to imagine the smallest bit of it.

Have you ever experienced a situation where someone separated from you, and then you heard about their life later on and thanked God you weren't with them anymore? They could have become a murderer, drug addict, or infected with some disease. The best thing they did for you was leaving you just like they did. The suffering didn't feel so great, but you're thanking God now. Nor are we to glory in other's misfortunes.

So you say that the person that left you was a millionaire. That doesn't mean they are happy, and you don't know how they really got to become one, so you'd still be in trouble if you were still with them. Lots of money, but can't sleep at night because you are afraid of someone knocking on the door or a phone call you didn't want to receive. You'd constantly have to look over your shoulder.

All things work out for our good, but we never want to accept the pain that we must endure to get to that point. It just hurts too badly. I guess that's the same thing the gold rings you are wearing are saying; they had to go through the hot fire and bear the pain to be melted just for you to wear and allow you to be able to say, "Isn't this ring beautiful?"

We are all getting melted down every day. This is to let us know that we are not whom we think we are. Our real beauty will unfold when we are tried and tested through the fire. Our testimony will be so true and vibrant that it will give someone who crosses our path just a little more strength to make it one step further in life. It is the anointing on our testimony that breaks the yoke!

It doesn't matter how or who helps you get to the top of the mountain; the key is to get there in honesty and peace. Listen to this: One time I broke up a relationship because I was just too madly in love. How was that for a clincher? This girl had my mind messed up. I couldn't eat; I was constantly worried about where she was and what she possibility could have been doing. I was just too jealous, until it almost drove me crazy. Believe it or not, she was basically innocent; it was my insecurity and immaturity that was whipping my brain.

I had the whole love thing twisted up. I started cheating on her, hoping this would take away some of the jealousy. It only made it worse. Seeking God was the only thing that started helping me. I cried out, "Lord, get this feeling out of me so I can live again."

I can also remember playing mental games, saying anything to turn off my heartache, such as "She hates my mother"; "she wants to kill me"; "she's nothing but a tramp."

I used another tactic that didn't have anything to do with love but I was sure it would work. I was very sick for about four months with migraine headaches that seemed like they came special delivery straight from hell. So I posted Bible scriptures all over the house, such as "By his stripes I'm healed," "The joy of the Lord is my strength," and many more. My place looked like a walking little Bible.

Thank God it worked. If you have to paste signs all over your house quoting positive scriptures, you do it. It is the power through the word of God that heals us. "He sent his word, and healed them, and delivered them from their destructions" (Ps. 107:20).

You will find yourself telling someone that you had to make up your mind and let go—and of course you'll be thanking God for giving you the strength; otherwise, you'd be in a real pickle. We are designed to go through tribulations; we can endure the pain, but it is all by faith.

> Therefore, having being justified by faith, we have peace with God through our Lord Jesus Christ, through whom also we have access by faith into this grace in which we stand, and rejoice in hope of the glory of God. Not only that, but we also glory in tribulations; knowing that tribulation produces perseverance; and perseverance, experience; character, and character hope. Now hope does not disappoint; because the love of God has been poured out in our hearts by the Holy Spirit who was given to us.
> (Rom. 5:1-5)

You wouldn't have patience had you not gone through some tribulations whereby you had to wait them out, regardless of the pain. It's just like a bad open cut: It's painful, but you have to wait for the healing, and by receiving air and space, that cut will heal automatically.

If a negative situation occurs again, it won't be as bad because within yourself you'll say, "I've gone through this before, and with the help of God I'll make it through this one too." Whatever the case may be, it will soon be over, and through God's love, you'll be at peace once again.

Our lives are like viewing an open country from an airplane. Looking down, all we see are valleys and mountains, peaks and high places. One day we're up, and the next day we're down, but thank God we can see the valleys and the mountains and that we know who will help us through them all. Go ahead and thank God, and never be ashamed of your past. We are all messed up in some form or fashion, and we all are still being worked upon.

> Do you know that the unrighteous will not inherit the kingdom of God? Do not be deceived. Neither fornicators, nor idolaters, nor adulterers, nor homo-sexuals, nor sodomites, nor thieves, nor covetous, nor drunkards, nor revilers, nor extortioners, will inherit the kingdom of God. Such were some of you; but you were washed, but you were sanctified, but you were justified in the name of the Lord Jesus, and by the Spirit of our God.
> (I Cor. 6:9)

Understand that our flesh and blood will not enter anyhow, because it is our Spirit. Our flesh and blood is too contaminated to enter. Do you have the Spirit of God? (ICor.15:50)

The above scripture says you were washed. Washing is a process. Trying to get dirt out of white clothing is a great process. It takes soaking and dipping. Then washing and ringing. Sometimes they are not still lily white and have to go back again. First you must except that the white clothing is dirty. It also says that you are justified. Just as if nothing happened. God is faithful if we would just ask Him. He already knows! Like the policeman as he watches you go through the red light. There's no need of lying as you receive your ticket. He already knows, and every now and then one just might let you off the hook. He was only doing his job. Romans 13:1—Let every soul be subject to the governing authorities. For there is no authority except from God, and the authorities that exist are appointed by God. Therefore whoever resists the authority resists the ordinance of God, and those who resist will bring judgment on themselves. For rulers are not a terror to good works, but to evil. Do you want to be unafraid of the authority: Do what is good, and you will have praise from the same.

We will make mistakes, but we have to forgive ourselves as God has forgiven us. It is because of our past and our experiences through Christ that we will help someone else whose path we may cross. Many times we just want to trust God only a little bit or when it's convenient, but God never changes—we do.

I remember a story about an old couple. When their relationship first started they would always take these long car rides, the wife as cuddly as she could be beside her husband—it almost looked like she was in his lap she was so close. The years went by and many conversations took place in this fine automobile; however, one day they got into a heated conversation, as the wife hadn't realized that for many months she'd been sitting closer to the passenger window.

"We are not close anymore," she told her husband. "I remember when I used to sit right under you and we would talk about everything. We were just so close." After listening for several minutes, the husband pulled the car over to the side of the road and said, "Yes, we were very close, but I never moved." That is just like God. He never moves. Jesus Christ is the same yesterday, today, and forever (Heb.13:1).

As you can see, there's always one that has to put the blame on someone else. In this case, the wife was the one who was constantly nagging and frustrated, moving closer and closer to the passenger door. If that had happened nowadays, he probably would have opened the door and let her fall out.

Once we give our testimony to others about our trials and tribulations and how the grace of God brought us out, we begin to feel and know once again that God is able to do exceedingly abundantly above all that we ask or think, according to the power that works in us, to Him be glory in the church by Christ Jesus to all generations, forever and ever. Amen. (Eph. 3:20)

IF YOU CAN WORK IT OUT

If there's a little hope left in the relationship and you both are seeking God about it, go for it! Caution: I did say if you *both* are seeking God!

If you both are *not* seeking God, you will continue to have problems. It would be as though only one of you was going to a marriage counselor, while the other one sat at home to see if it would work. Try going to a marriage counselor that hasn't been married. He'll have plenty of book advice to give you. What hands on experience can they give you? We used to say, "If you can't get along, get it on!"

If God was not in favor of the relationship from the beginning, you can stay with each other for the next twenty years and remain mad with the world—because nothing will work. Consider where you met them, you just might need to take them back and dump him or her off and pray that one-day they'll be straightened out. You may catch the fish, but will have a heck of a time cleaning him.

Problems do occur in relationships, but if they are constantly reoccurring, you might as well come to grips and take inventory. Ask yourself, "Who is this killing? Me or them?" As the old saying goes, "If you keep doing what you're doing, you'll keep getting what you're getting."

Each of you knows exactly what the problem is, but you are refusing to admit it. These problems can range from personality swings to unsatisfied sex. I don't know everyone in the world, but if you are not giving a person what he or she wants, it won't be before long they will find it somewhere—with or without you. It's like blowing air in a balloon. It can only take so much before it burst.

If the relationship can sincerely be made into something positive and meaningful, then it may work out for your good. If so, you can tell others the immediate changes you had to make in order to keep the relationship.

If both parties won't bend, however, one will look like the bow and the other one will look like the arrow. Don't keep beating a dead horse; he can only die once, and it's up to God to do the resurrecting.

Meanwhile, go seek what God has in store for you to do and who to be with, if any one at all.

TAKE YOUR MEDICINE

We can visit the family doctor week after week hoping to become healthy. The doctor gives us a prescription to be filled. After filling it, we can take the bottle and set it on the dresser without taking any of the medicine and wonder why it is not working. If it doesn't get down on the inside, it will never work.

In the same sense, we can look at the Bible and say all year long, "I do not understand it because it is so confusing." I promise you that if you ask God, through faith he will help you understand. There are all types of new translations now. If you are not a reader, there's still no excuse. You can listen to it on tape. There is some bible tapes that are excellent with all the different dramatic voices, as though you are listening to a story. People have been studying and preaching the bible for years and still don't understand parts of it until God gives them revelation. Relax, the bible is not having a brain contest.

Remember when our parents would tell us that we would understand it better by and by? God wants you to get the word deep on the inside, as though you were eating it. Although it makes you bitter and causes you to think and repent, it will be a sweet testimony out of your mouth. It's just like medicine: Even though it doesn't taste good, it still works.

As John explains, "So I went to the angel and said to him, "Give me the little book." Then he said to me, "Take and eat it; and it will make your stomach bitter, but it will be as sweet as honey in your mouth (Rev. 10:9)."

Ask God to lead you and guide you where you should go

and hear the word. Remember you have not because you did not ask (James 4:2).

As you hear the word of God, it will start changing your mind about things. There's nothing like a little gospel medicine. If you think ALEVE® works, you should try Jesus—and he doesn't charge.

When we are very weak, we must pull ourselves up and get some medicine. It's like calling 911; this is an emergency. Because we are in such a hurry for this quick healing, we think God has forgotten about us. We tell the microwave oven to hurry up. When we are in a hurry, it's similar to an emergency room that takes the worse cases first, while we wait and suffer. Believe it or not, when the nurses are looking at you, they have an idea of how much you can endure, and so does Jesus.

When we are going through problems in life, we never know whom God has set in our paths to say the right words at the right time. "A word fitly spoken is like apples of gold in settings of silver" (Prov. 25:11). Wouldn't that make a beautiful picture? That's how the word of God sounds when He speaks to us, whether personally or through someone else. The word will fit the situation and will make you think and understand at that time.

If you need healing you don't need anyone talking to you about financial blessings.

There is a time for everything in our lives. I have always said that God made the first computer. He programmed everything and then pushed "run." Everything in the Bible and in our lives is taking place today, and it won't stop until the program is "complete." Being confident of this very thing, that He who has begun a good work in you will complete it until the day of Jesus Christ (Phil.1:6). Who better than Solomon to tell us about the right time?

To everything there is a season, and a time to every purpose
under the heaven;
A time to be born, and a time to die;
A time to plant and a time to pluck up that which is
planted;
A time to kill, and a time to heal;
A time to break down and a time to build up;
A time to weep, and a time to laugh;
A time to mourn and a time to dance;
A time to cast away stones, and a time to gather stones
together;
A time to embrace, and a time to refrain from embracing;
A time to get, and a time to lose;
A time to keep, and a time to cast away;
A time to rend, and a time to sew;
A time to keep silence and a time to speak;
A time to love, and a time to hate;
A time of war, and a time of peace. (Eccles. 3:1)

Whatever you are going through, it's just your time! You
can overcome it! Trust me on this one: The Devil will never tell
you anything that will work in your favor. He will never tell you
to hold on and have faith!

I heard a little story once that the Devil was fighting against
God's word to those who hadn't accepted Christ. He came to realize that his strategy was not working as effective as he wanted
to. So he came up with another plan. He would use people to tell
others, that Jesus was true and the word of God was true, but
they had plenty of time to accept Jesus. Now that's what you call
a slick Devil. Procrastination is the killer of all dreams.

Nothing good comes from the Devil. If anything he will
tell you to kill yourself, that you can't keep anyone, that you'll

never make it in life, that he or she found someone better, and that you're not going to be anything. Whose report will you believe? I shall believe the report of the Lord! I can do all things through Christ who strengthens me (Phil.4:13).

LOVE MEANS NEVER HAVING TO SAY, "I'M SORRY"

Who in the world thought of that? When you're in love, all you do is say you're sorry; when it's over, you're saying, "I am sorry that I allowed you to waste my time."

We might think it was a waste, but more than likely it was beneficial and taught us something. Learning is an everyday process. It's not all going to be apple pie, but know that sometimes you have to get a little lemon custard.

Sometimes we use these little clichés and don't really understand them because of how some sentimental person used them. "Love means never having to say you're sorry" is almost as bad as "What you don't know can't hurt you." If you think about it, what you don't know can almost destroy your life, especially if you're in a relationship that is not going anywhere.

Many times in a relationship, we hate to say that we're sorry, and it is just two little words. Of course, sometimes we hate saying that we're sorry because of the other person's response: "Is that all you have to say?" Unfortunately that is it. You already know what happened so what else is there to say?

I recall a pastor stating that a member gave a large amount of money to his church, and of course he said, "Thank you." When he thought about church members and how some might try to persuade pastors to do certain things because of their contributions, he stated that his obligation and debt was paid when he simply said, "Thank you." Right is right and wrong is wrong regardless of how much you give. That is what has torn up churches today because of favoritism and unfair decisions.

Some people have different ways of saying they're sorry without actually saying it. For example, you might be taken to dinner or receive a gift. A nice non-verbal way of saying "I'm sorry" because of the guilt, but nothing fits the bill other than to say it regardless if the other individual doesn't want to accept it. The healing process has to start somewhere, and saying "I'm sorry" is a good introduction to the end of a good performance.

You can't win a person's trust back by continuing buying gifts. It's not that you have to make Christmas everyday. After-all Santa Claus gets tired too. Now you feel obligated to buy. Remember there's no price-tag on forgiveness.

Not only that, what are you going to do if you run out of money? Suppose they still leave. The next thing you would say is, "Had I known that, I could have saved my money."

Real forgiveness takes the strength of God.

Had it been left to us the person would never get it. God has to show us our own evil ways and short comings for us to understand. We will be challenged in situations hoping others will forgive us. As read in Matthew 18:21—Then Peter came to Him and said, "Lord, how often shall my brother sin against me, and I forgive him? Up to seven times?"

Jesus said to him, "I do not say to you, up to seven times, but up to seventy times seven." That's four hundred and ninety times. We're still holding grudges towards people who have only hurt us once.

LOST AND FOUND

You lost yourself and found someone you didn't know, and now you think that you have to start all over again. This may be true, but thank God for giving you the wisdom and the strength to start over.

We are nothing but a bag of feelings: we cry; we laugh; we get depressed and we get angry. We wake up in the morning with this bag and have no idea what we're going to pull out in the course of a day.

It is the same way with a relationship: We don't know what type of feelings the other person has in his or her bag until it is revealed or leaks out. When it does, we are in shock and have to go pull a feeling out of our bag. Which one will we choose then? The sad feeling of rejection and pain, or the feeling of peace because now you know the truth?

We not only lose our sense of self in a relationship, but when it is devastating enough, we lose weight, hair, and self-esteem. Some may gain weight, but the point is that something happens physically. "All things work together for the good to him that love the Lord" (Rom. 8:28). We sometimes don't see it; we just feel it, and most times it isn't pleasant if we don't see it coming.

Have you ever heard about a marriage where the husband comes home and out of the clear blue sky and says he wants a divorce? The wife never saw the signs coming; she just went along like everything was fine. Staying out late and not doing things together anymore are sure signs that someone is getting pretty bored. Whether or not you personally can pick up on these signs and restore the marriage, I don't have the slightest idea. Search your heart.

Sometimes we lose a relationship but find peace and happiness. It's not necessarily that you want anyone else; it's simply that you don't have to listen to anyone's voice but your own. You might miss some of the things the person did, but all things will work out so long as you know what to do. It's like backing a cat in a corner, he will come out!

Many times, the spouse that is left behind has no idea how much money is in the bank or how or where to pay the bills; they just went along for the ride without paying attention to the potholes or the flowers along the way.

God is still able. I suppose you're asking, "Able to do what?" He's able to give you strength and a mind to carry on and make it. You trusted the other individual, so try trusting God now; see how long He will stay.

There are three reasons why you will go to the "Relationship Lost and Found": (1) To drop your emotions off on everyone around you, (2) To pick up your pride and embarrassment and go on, and (3) To see if the person is there waiting for you, thinking that it was just a phase they were going through when they said they wanted to end the relationship.

Finally, after many days and no phone calls, it hits you that you are on your own. So you make a list in your mind of what you're going to do:

1. I'm going to attend church more.
2. I'm going to start socializing more.
3. I'm going to start snooping around his or her apartment to see if there's someone else.

4. I'm just going to stay home and get depressed and eat all day.
5. I'm going to stop dressing up.

Truly the list can go on and on. You would have to decide whether or not to go in a positive or negative direction. Remember it's easier to roll down a hill than to go up it. With God's help you will be able to pull up the hill again. The negative decision would only make things worse, sort of going down the hill; it would get to the point that not even friends would want to be around you because they were tired of the same old story. A cassette tape will eventually wear out if you play it long enough.

All you need is at least one positive person in your life that will help and guide you through these trials. Another depressed person will only make things worse. What direction will you be stepping toward? A positive or negative one?

As said many times: Misery loves company.

Be careful: Just because you decide to step in a positive direction doesn't mean that negativity will not come along. It can even come from friends: "You sure are out there fast"; "You didn't give them a chance to leave." Deep down inside, however, you know what you're doing. That's why you may have to get around people that are not aware of the situation at all and are only interested in having a good time.

The only possible alarm that I could think of is to beware of the person who has already had three or four husbands or wives. It's not that God can't change their pattern because there is nothing impossible for Him. Until you get to know God and able to discern, beware! A leopard may never change his spots, but he sure can change his territory.

MARRIAGE TONIGHT, PREGNANT
IN THE MORNING

Our almighty God ordains marriage: "What God has joined together let no man put asunder" (Matt. 19:6). I never thought I would be the one to say a person should wait awhile before they start having children, but it is so very true.

If your relationship or marriage is not one that is true and ordained by God, you are in store for a real treat. As it is said, it should be God joining us together, not man. If there is any doubt, *don't do it.*

I am aware that people change to some degree, but what you have now is the biggest part of them. In our hearts, we want a perfect relationship, and so we think that if the person changes a few things, then they'll be as madly in love with us as we are with them. Don't rack your brain, but you can't force someone to love you. You'll never get that elephant in the closet.

Another situation may be that a woman feels she can trap a man into marrying her by getting pregnant. That's all dandy, but guess what? Marriages end every day and that will be one more to add to the list and a baby left behind.

We often play tricks with our inner spirit, but the truth will eventually come out. You can really tell if the two of you feel the same way about each other. No matter how hard you pray a square will never fit into a circle—unless it is carved down.

Both need to see the same thing. Same as a sculptor:

You may see a block of wood and he may see the bust of a famous person.

Sometimes having a child too soon in a marriage that you are not sure about to begin with tends to take the concentration off of what is—or isn't—really there. Many couples don't even understand each other or know how to enjoy each other's company, when along comes the little bambino needing all of the attention. Then the shoving of the responsibility off onto one another begins, and the next thing they know only one parent is around for the rest of the baby's life.

What does the child think about this? Well, he's not sure because the parents haven't pumped negativity about each other into his mind yet. When they do, however, the child will be filled with mixed emotions.

The child may also be thinking, "Mommy doesn't like me because part of the man that she hates is in me and this causes shame. The same child may want to call the other parent but doesn't because the parent the child is staying with will view the behavior as taking sides and maybe mistreat the child as a result.

I used to work in a department store, and I'll never forget the day that my manager brought her child in. Something happened and the young child busted out laughing, which embarrassed the manager, who in a rage said, "You stop laughing like that. You laugh just like your father." Of course, the child stopped.

All too often, children who are products of divorces are taught to dislike the other parent. Sometimes the parent who doesn't live with the child becomes distant because of the ex's constant bitter comments when present or over the telephone. Because the absent parent doesn't want to hear it, any type of relationship with the child is lost. Tell me: Who loses?

Once a child enters the picture, a whole new atmosphere exists. It's like having a glass of white milk and putting a tablespoon of chocolate syrup in it. The white milk is still there, but the chocolate has changed the taste and the color. Wait if you can to have children.

The picture of the American family is of a husband, wife, daughter, and son, but it's just that: a picture. Just wait until it comes alive. Then tell me what you really see in America. Especially since the government has taken over the corporal punishment laws.

WHAT ABOUT MY CHILD?

Well, what about him? So you are depressed now that you are left with a child? One sure thing about life, as much as we hate to face it, is that men are dogs and women are cats! May the best animal win!

Now, I know that sounds pretty unpleasant, but one thing about God is that He already knew when the child was coming and when the man was going to leave. Let me not be so cold on the man; there are some women who leave their children too. Whatever the reason for the separation, there's a child and an ex-relationship.

God forgives all of our mistakes and getting pregnant is one of them, but the child still has to be taken care of. That's the extra suitcase we hadn't planned on taking on the trip. You might not think it's so depressing that the other party left, but the fact that the child looks and acts just like them might get on your nerves. At times, you might still want that presence of the other parent.

Lashing out, name-calling, hating the other individual, and wanting to drain them for child support will never bring your once-loving relationship back. If anything, it will keep him or her further away. Who in the world would want to be around somebody saying such things?

In such circumstances, the person will possibly pay the child support but never see the child. Sometimes there is too much bitterness to handle. Some ex-spouses will play their greedy games and try to get the child to ask the absent parent for more money. What if the person that left doesn't have any money? It's especially sad when the spouse wanting more money is financially capable of taking care of the child already. It is not to say that the other partner should not do their share. What if they are unable to at the time? Do you make them hate you and despise you? After all I don't think they would have left had they not felt you were able to handle things. Only God knows.

A person without an understanding what is going on in the other person's life, usually the woman, would say, "Well, he needs to pay. If he wasn't able to take care of them, then he shouldn't of made them." True enough, but he can justly turn around and say, "If she'd been on birth control, neither one of us would have had to worry."

This conversation could go on forever, everyone blaming the other; it's just like prejudice. All the while, the parents' negativity gets planted in the child's suffering and confused head. If a child feels negative about a parent who is not around, I guarantee you that a lot of negativity has been said by the parent who is around. One day, however, it will all come back to them. I recall a lady calling her fifteen year old daughter a Bitch. The daughter replied, "I'm just like you."

People are making mistakes every day by having children. One mistake is okay, but it's a big problem when there are three or four mistakes and no marriage. After the first child, if the mother is not married, the state should mandate that her tubes automatically be tied.

Many women are tricking men by getting pregnant. It is to trap the man or get some money. What would probably stop that is creating a law that makes a man not liable for child support if a woman is over eighteen and gets pregnant without being married. I guarantee you that many of these women would think twice about getting pregnant.

A man doesn't even have a chance with the way the government is set up now; the woman is usually sided with even though she often is the creator of the problem in the first place—just ask Eve. The Devil knows that the man will be of no use to anyone if burdened down and frustrated. The government is very good at pressuring men about things they shouldn't, yet women play on these tactics, not realizing that they are weakening the men more every day. God forbid if he's henpecked. You can see the embarrassment on his face when his mate scolds him in public. In other words she is saying, "I wear the pants, you just buy them."

Nagging alone is enough to drive someone crazy. "It is better to dwell in the corner of the house top, than with a brawling woman in a wide house…. It is better to dwell in the wilderness, than with a contentious and angry woman" (Prov. 21:19). On the other hand, "A man must understand that a man who is born of a woman is of few days, and full of trouble" (Job 14:1).

I'm not trying to be a woman basher, but why would you want to get pregnant and go through the pain and agony for nine months of having a child for someone that you are not even sure is going to be there? As far as that is concerned, no one can be sure about anyone being there, even if it's a Christian marriage—but at least you would have a better chance. Of course that statement sounds good. However, there are just as many Christians getting divorces as so called non-Christians.

Don't worry if the person leaves. Take care of your child. Love your child. You may be raising a millionaire. If you are not wise you may be raising a nut. Everything happens for a reason, and God has all the answers. Don't step in and try to get vengeance, because vengeance will repeat itself. That child will be taken care of. "Beloved, do not avenge yourselves, but rather give place to wrath: for it is written, Vengeance is mine; I will repay, says the Lord" (Rom. 12:19).

God says, "All souls are mine" (Ezek. 18:4). What better hands can the two of you be in? You are left behind but not alone. As David said, "If I ascend into heaven, you are there: if I make my bed in hell, behold, you are there" (Ps. 139:8).

FINISHED, BUT WON'T FACE IT

Some good things must come to an end, and so must bad things. Even though we've been talking about how to get over past relationships after you have separated, there is another case we must also face: Being in a state of denial can be extremely dangerous.

When you fuss about and nit-pick each other all day it's because you think that you are in love but you're not; you are just addicted to one another. I'm sure that there are all kinds of love, but if you call that love, no wonder no one wants it. It gets to the point where you can't wait for them to get home so that you will have something to fuss about, and of course the other person is already thinking about what's behind the front door.

You both are finished with the relationship, but you won't face it. You'd rather go on and act like it's okay. You're probably not even attempting to go out with friends anymore for fear that your partner will say something smart and make you not want to go at all.

You may be a busy person and your partner isn't. So, to them you are just too busy and need to slow down. To you, they need to get up off of their butt and do something. Have you ever wondered why some couples stay together so long? Well, when one works days and the other works nights, there's little time for communication. Usually this occurs with couples that have been together a long time; the love bug is sort of tired, so it doesn't make any difference when they work.

Truckers who date get along well because they only have

to see one another one or two weeks out of the month, if that. Some of these cases work and some don't, but compatibility is always the key.

Some start off like they are in a so-called compatible relationship, but after a while the true person will come out. It's like buying a new shirt in the store. It fits and looks well while in the store. However when you get the shirt home you're ready to take it back to get a refund because it doesn't look the same on at your place. In relationships what was okay at first begins to be annoying; what was once thought of as cute winds up sending a person's blood pressure through the roof and his or her nose up in the air every time it occurs.

You can raise a dog with a chicken, but one-day when the dog gets mad, there goes the chicken. What was once a friend now may look like a problem or a meal, especially if the dog is not being fed.

If a couple don't feed each other, there will definitely be a problem. For example, you might talk to your friends on the phone constantly but not have two words to say to your mate. If there's nothing to talk about, then that's a good sign that what you thought was there is not, or what was there has lost its vigor. You're throwing money in the wishing well, but at night someone comes and digs it out. There is just false hope.

Another thing that happens is that a person begins to not look as attractive as you thought they were. A male could have started out with a young lady that had a figure like a Coca-Cola® bottle, and now it's like a gallon of milk. That's because instead of nipping the weight in the bud, you started looking elsewhere because you were into the physical aspect of the relationship. The same could happen in reverse with a female with a very good-looking man that changes.

Others become very jealous, another sign that you are not

compatible. When a person has to explain how they feel about their mate, often times it will go something like this: "I love him but ...," The funny thing about it is there's a lot of information that is negative after saying "but." The only thing I know regarding the "but" is that you have a problem, "but" you won't deal with it.

Take this test: How do you feel when they are not around? Peaceful, huh? It wouldn't be bad if they stay gone at this point, once you have realized who they are. The only thing you might be enjoying is sex, and that's only a possibility. Think about it: If this person could not perform sexually, would you still be willing to stay with them?

Sometimes your head will start hurting just talking about them, yet you continue to stay there.

You'll go complaining about your head hurting just to keep from having sex.

I recall a joke the comedian Richard Pryor told many years ago. There was a woman who hated having sex with her husband. So every time they would get in the bed she would say that her period was on. After several months of this her husband replied: "Girl, you're going to bleed to death aren't you?"

Neither of you are happy; you just tolerate one another. When you see someone else you're attracted to, you'll say to yourself, "I wish my current partner would just leave"—even though you know that they aren't going anywhere, because you're not. Gladys Knight used to sing, "Neither one of us wants to be the first to say good-bye." Somebody better hurry up and say something because you are wasting your time. Don't risk the chance of waking up and realizing you're too old to think about moving. As I heard one person say that it's nothing wrong with being old, it's just so inconvenient. Same as: "What I use to do all day, now it takes all day for me to do."

In reality if there's no lovemaking or compassionate feelings you have already said good-bye, but just haven't left physically. Have you ever heard the expression, "He's already dead, but just haven't lied down."

I often think about relationships where couples live together for years and never get married. In other words, "I love you enough to stay with you but not enough to marry you." Marriage holds a definite responsibility, which is probably what many are afraid of. Marriages should be like drivers' licenses: If you don't get along, you don't get them renewed, and all is well.

Your relationship is finished when there is no joy or happiness and when you've been hoping for months—even years—that one of you will move. It's like you're in jail and the key is on the wall, but you can't seem to reach it, so you keep stretching and stretching but the key doesn't get any closer. As though someone keeps moving the wall back further.

Maybe you've started drinking, smoking cigarettes or marijuana thinking that will heal the problem. It won't. By doing this, you're only encouraging your partner to walk out the door, leaving you behind as a depressed, lonely, and unwise alcoholic full of smoke.

Of course, you would say, "He drove me to drink." If that's the case, why couldn't he or she drive you to pick up your suitcase and leave? You just thought drinking or drugs would make it easier for you to tolerate, but now you are addicted. How long did it take for you to get addicted? You've also cried continuously but you never saw his tears because he was crying on the inside.

Here's a joke for you: A wife was playing the lotto and she won a million dollars. She went flying home, pulled up in the driveway, and parked her car. She ran in the house saying, "Honey! Pack the suitcases!" He asked, "Where are we going?" and she replied, "Nowhere. I want you to get the hell out of here."

You never know what will cause a person to make up their mind to separate. Believe it or not, money can make you do it too. Sometimes people put up with one another because of financial responsibility. I would rather make payments on that responsibility and get out of there while I was sane; you can't work when you go insane. Think about it! When it comes to finances most people are stressed out anyway. Why be in a negative relationship and broke too? As you know finances is the number one reason for divorce. If you don't have about six months of savings for all of your expenses in case of emergency you are mentally stressed out. One person's salary will not take care of all the bills. The shocking part is when you were single you had one job, living alone and making it. Now you're together and each of you have two jobs. When do you spend time with each other? As the old saying goes "I can do bad all by myself." Remember at first you two were so in love. The average person is two paychecks away from poverty. Some are only one paycheck away and being evicted as I speak. The real bad cases are only one day away. They can't take off one day of work for fear of a day's lost wages. Now ask me if you need to be in that relationship if you're not in love?

After leaving a job with all sorts of people with their hang-ups, traveling on the dangerous roads, attending churches with heavy financial responsibilities and dealing with outside family issues, who wants to come home to a negative house? That is the spot you should at least be able to settle down for a little peace. Maybe for those who can't get peace at home spend much time in the bathroom alone calling it their secret and quiet place. In other words, "God just give me one minute of peace before I go crazy." As the scripture says, Thou will keep him in perfect peace, whose mind is stayed on thee, because he trusts in thee (Isa.26:3).

How much longer can you stay? God forbids if infidelity creeps in. That will be the main subject every time a problem arrives unless real forgiveness in the heart has taken place. Usually the one that has committed the crime can't understand why the other person doesn't get over it immediately because at least they were told the truth. Or did they get caught? As Proverbs 18:19 reads: A brother offended is harder to win than a strong city. People don't plan to fail in life; they just fail to plan. If your relationship is draining you, you had better get to planning! If not, before long you will be saying, "I knew this was going to happen." Better known as that inner gut feeling. If you don't have a secret stash of savings, you had better start one. Suffer now or suffer later. It's not to say you don't have faith, but make sure it's not blind faith.

Realize that there is only one you, and you only get one computer chip in your brain. In this chip is every program you need to live in this world. The chip that holds all of your religious beliefs are there, too; you probably just haven't tapped into it yet. All of your desires and aspirations in life are on that chip.

You really know right from wrong, although you're not perfect. You even see some good in that partner of yours, but you know they're not good for you. It can be to the point that this other person is not doing any wrong at all—a good provider and lover and all of that—but something in your spirit doesn't click, and it turns out that you're the problem. Regardless of the case, your honesty is on that chip.

What has happened in the relationship is that a virus entered the program and for some reason you can't get it out. In many cases it was there already. It has gone through the chip in your brain, leaving you completely frustrated. The only way you can get rid of this virus is through God and getting another program.

Happiness is a privilege. Joy is an honor. Love is a necessity. Depression and frustration are curses. When we're in a negative relationship, we constantly curse ourselves out, and we do a good job of it. Who can beat us up better than ourselves? We know the answer, but we will torment ourselves until we totally crack up and reach the point where we are considered the demon in the relationship.

Once again, somebody has to start playing checkers and make a move. If you want to crown yourself, let the move be with wisdom.

SLEEPING WITH THE ENEMY

If night after night you go to bed with someone who is hostile toward you, all you have done is conditioned yourself to sleep with the enemy. He or she has been set there just to make you unhappy, and this can go on for years. They have taken your joy and even your desire to live; you just can't wait until you die. That's the strategy of the enemy because he or she can't wait either, whatever it takes for you to get out of their life.

Remember one thing about the enemy: He always wants to return to the scene of the crime. Many can't leave because of the materialistic aspect, but what difference does it make? You're not happy anyhow. You're surrounded around beautiful things that you can't enjoy plus the cost of upkeep.

In this case, someone has to make up his or her mind to talk or to leave. No one should have to deal with foolish people all day at work, and then come home to more foolishness. Where is the peace? Your enemy will go on day after day feeling nothing.

You have but one life, and many times we have to ask God for forgiveness and run for our life because that's the only one we get here on earth. Your enemy has the potential of subconsciously making you the person you really should be. Trials come to make you strong. Are you strong enough to leave and accept that they are gone?

Although Rome wasn't built in a day, the thought of building it could have only taken a minute. With your one minute, you have to make a decision about how you want to live—in misery or happiness. Which direction are you headed for?

You can't take the roller coaster ride unless you hop in the cart. It can be frightening and sometimes fun.

If you committed suicide, do you think you or the other person would have won? God would probably be wondering why you didn't consult Him about it. You see, God made man and he also made the devil but the devil tried to mold man and thought that you would accept him just to make your life miserable. It is only God that gives us strength to endure all situations. Everything starts off good, but something happens along the way. The Devil can make a day miserable, but he can't make a day.

As stated, all trials come to make us strong. The discomfort we have for a little while does not outweigh the benefits we'll receive after we've learned or achieved a goal. For example going to college four years and staying up late many nights studying may be a discomfort, but you graduated. It doesn't matter what your age may be!

Therefore we do not lose heart. Even though our outward man is perishing, yet the inward man is being renewed day by day. For our light affliction, which is but for a moment, is working for us a far more exceeding and eternal weight of glory, while we do not look at the things which are seen, but at the things which are not seen. For the things which are seen are temporary, but the things which are not seen are eternal (2Cor.4:16-18).

SORRY, BUT YOU'RE NEVER TOO OLD

Sorry, but you're never too old to go through pain and suffering that results from someone deciding to leave you. You're also never too old to find happiness, love, and peace. Our outer appearances change, but our hearts remain the same. The person on the inside of you can be taller, stronger and wiser if we'd listen to him. He's just sitting down waiting to be called.

I wouldn't care if you were ninety years old; God has a companion for you if you're seeking one.

I heard the funniest thing in church when someone said that a certain lady mentioned that the Lord had told her that this particular deacon was going to be her husband. Another lady replied, "Well the Lord better tell him too."

We have said that we are too old for this and too old for that, but the Bible says: "We are snared by the words of our mouth" (Prov.6: 2).

Abusive relationships occur with the old as well as the young. We often don't imagine an old man and woman arguing and physically fighting, but it happens. The weaker party believes that they have nowhere to go, so they sit and deal with what is going on around them.

How sad it is that older people do not get the attention that they need from such a wealthy society. Rest homes are expensive, and churches and families often don't have enough time. So what do the elderly do? They have no choice but to trust in God that soon this too will be over.

By faith they can pack their one little suitcase, walk out the door, and hope that maybe someone will take them in. No one needs to suffer physically or mentally. If they take that one step and ask God, without a shadow of a doubt someone, somewhere, will come to the rescue—he's that kind of God.

Many times the elderly will not get involved in senior-citizen programs, but if strength is not used, it will be lost. For bodily exercise profits a little, but godliness is profitable for all things (1Tim.4:7). This lets me know that exercise does profit. Sometimes we have to try to force this group of people to get involved in activities, especially if they lose someone they cared for, whether by death or by choice. We all have feelings regardless of age—pain is pain—but remember the happiness we lost can be restored with enjoying one day at a time.

Life has no rewind buttons, only forward.

Sometimes placing affirmation cards around the house builds up your hope and desires, such as: "The joy of the Lord is my strength" or "I can do all things through Christ who strengthens me." Try it. It's the simple and little things in life that get big results.

But God has chosen the foolish things of the world to put to shame the wise, and God has chosen the weak things of the world to put to shame the things which are mighty; and the base things of the world and the things which are despised God has chosen, and the things which are not, to bring to nothing the things that are, that no flesh should glory in His presence. Of Him you are in Christ Jesus, who became for us wisdom from God—and righteousness and sanctification and redemption—that, as it is written, *He who glories, let him glory in the Lord."* (1Cor.1:27-31)

DON'T BE SELFISH

Have you ever been in a selfish situation or you were "the selfish situation?" Say, you didn't want the person, but you didn't want them to have anyone else? How shrewd can you be? You are only in the way of yourself and the other person.

If you are concerned about the person and love them with an unconditional heart, regardless of your selfishness, jealousy, and anything else, only God can help you. Remember that love is selfish, and when it is rejected it wants to rebel. Whitney Houston sang it best in the movie *The Bodyguard*:

If I should stay
I would only be in the way
So I'll go, but I know, that I'll think
of you every step of the way
I'll always love you

You have to understand that if you don't want to be with the person, or the person doesn't want to be with you, your feelings and emotions are only in the way. Yes, you will always think about them; once you've taken part of the forbidden fruit; your eyes are truly open. You'll just have to learn to love them from a distance. Now that's a real distant lover!

All of the selfishness you are building up is only going to lead you to high blood pressure and a possible heart attack. Going through pain from a relationship is just like going to jail: Just make up in your mind that you have to serve the time. This "time" is the pain that you will have to endure. Have you ever stumped your toe and cursed? After a while the pain will go away, but at that moment you are cursing like a sailor.

If you follow the steps of Christ and try to learn about his love, you just might get out quicker on good behavior. The longer you sit in the room and look at the four walls, the larger and taller they will become. Eventually it will take a bulldozer to get through to you to help you realize that flowers are still blooming and the sea is still a beautiful blue outside those walls.

Sit by a lake and talk to God. He will meet you in the storm, but the water that settles will be at peace.

As an old man once said: "I never knew how beautiful flowers were on the side of the road until I had to walk because I was too old to drive."

I GUESS I'LL TRY THE GUILT TRIP

Back into your bag of tricks again, huh? I understand the pain and the frustration, but now you're trying to make the person feel guilty for leaving you. You're thinking of all that you have done together, your beautiful house, nice cars, and successful business.

You're saying, "You know we have worked through thick and thin together. Remember how I helped you through college and neither of us had much money or food to eat during that time? How you and my parents get along so well and my kid brother just loves you? Look at your daughter. She needs you, and she looks just like you, but you're going to throw it all out of the door just like that."

The next thing you know you're taking it out on yourself: "I'm not good enough for anyone"; "I'm stupid and ugly"; "I don't have a degree because I had to quit school at a young age and work and help the family"; "I know I'm in the way of your business"; "My mother's sick."

You have thought of all the things to say. You are all bound up with the worries of this world, which will never last. You're crying again after thinking about all that you are about to lose. Those tears, however, are tears of washing; after while you will want to cry but there will be no tears, just pain.

Do not love the world, or the things in the world. If anyone loves the world, the love of the Father is not in him. For all that is in the world—the lust of the flesh,

and the lust of the eyes, and the pride of life—is not
of the Father but is of the world.
The world is passing away, and the lust of it:
but he who does the will of God abides forever.
(IJohn 2:15)

Once you pull through all that you're going through,
knowing God has allowed you to go through things for a reason,
you will hold your head up and look toward the hill from which
your help came, which was from the Lord (Ps.121:2). Just think
about it! After you wept, had all of your tantrums, and dished
out dozens of guilt trips, guess what? The person still left you!

Now you're feeling really depressed and embarrassed. The
neighbors saw you out on the front lawn crawling on your knees
and shouting, "Please don't go! I love you!" I know you love him
or her, but they don't want to stay, and you'll just have to respect
that. As one mountain said to the other, "You'll get over it."

You might as well get up off the grass and wash your knees
because the person that left you is probably saying, "Had I
stayed with her longer, I guess she would have jumped off of the
bridge next, and I don't think she'd feel too good when she hit
the bottom."

ONE LAST CRY

Pop artist Brian McKnight sends a clear message in his song entitled "One Last Cry":

Believe it or not you should get yours. Sometimes it can be a true cleansing, because you have really felt and know without a doubt that it is all over. Cry until you can't cry any more. With those tears come pain, hurt, disappointment, jealousy and any other thing that may have hurt you. After the bucket is emptied with that one last cry what will you fill your buckets with? Water that sits in the sun will dry up. Take those tears and sit out on the beach and enjoy the sunshine.

The choice is yours. You're probably asking, "What am I going to do?" I'll tell you what you're going to do: You're going to get up and live like you're new to the town. It is a new day that you have never seen before, and you have no idea of the many good things God will be placing in your life now that you have decided to ask for His help. God's not slow; he just does a thorough job. He's into detail work. He just doesn't wash the outside of your car. He cleanses the inside as well. God keeps going forward. Didn't I just tell you a few paragraphs ago that life doesn't come with a rewind button, but misery does.

Have you ever thought you were out of a relationship, but it was never finished? The last conversation was never dealt with, and you did not get a chance to get your one last cry. You went through several relationships afterwards, but you kept thinking about this person year after year, never finalized anything.

Well, it happened to me, too. I got out of a relationship

where we both had gone totally cuckoo. We were too scared to call one another because so many people had gotten involved with the outcome. After seven years, I tracked down her phone number; we talked for five hours—and I was living in another state. That phone bill was worth it; and it was before they had all of these specials.

After hanging up, I had my one last cry. I was *so* hurt because I realized that I could have saved the relationship. I'm better now. Can't cry over spilled milk—you just go get another cow!

THAT THORN IN THE FLESH

To the Bible readers: Do you recall Paul saying,

"Lest I should be exalted above measure by the abundance of the revelations, a thorn in the flesh was given to me, a messenger of Satan to buffet me, lest I be exalted above measure. Concerning this thing I pleaded with the Lord three times that it might depart from me, and he said to me, "My grace is sufficient for you: for My strength is made perfect in weakness" (2 Cor. 12:7)?

It was never said specifically what this thorn was, but some believe it was some type of sickness or acute pain. Nevertheless, Paul consulted the Lord about it, and the Lord said His grace was sufficient, that it was all he needed. Paul believed that this thorn was not removed so that it would keep him humble.

Many times when two separate in a relationship, there is a thorn left that serves as a constant reminder of what once was. It can be in the form of a child, a bruise, or a lovely memory, but this thorn will always be there, and sometimes it will keep us humble. It will keep us from judging others because of our own condition or past experiences that have the potential to be exposed.

Whatever your thorn represents, be confident that God's grace is sufficient and all that you need at this day and time. Things can always be worse. Thank God that your torture ends here. Now it's time to go ahead and believe God is still there.

We have so many "whys" in life; sometimes they are answered, and other times they are not. We don't see the end result until down the road when we realize that our past experiences can help someone else whose condition is worse. Remember the saying: "I stopped complaining that I had no new shoes when I met a man who had no feet."

Often we carry a lot of problems in our suitcases from the last relationship we were in. Your thorn in the flesh may be the suitcase itself, which may very well be **you.** Allow the inside to become emptied so that you may restore it with exciting and positive things. When we change from the inside, the outside doesn't look as bad as you think. Love yourself; take care of yourself; and learn to love others regardless if they can't be with you.

The bottom line is: Be fair. Would *you* want to stay somewhere that you didn't want to be? If *you* were leaving, how would you have done it differently? Free is Free.

In life, we all come across different teachers, but we all end up with the same results. We had to learn. We're still alone with a thorn in the flesh, but God's grace is sufficient. We need to stop repeating the same patterns which causes us stress. How is it that we have time to do something over, but don't have time to do it right!

YOU MUST ENROLL

Have you ever had the desire to be a doctor, lawyer, cosmetologist, teacher, or anything profession? You know as well as I that there are many things you can learn on your own, but today's society wants you to have a piece of paper, better known as some type of degree.

In obtaining this degree, you first have to fill out a school application and give the proper information, after which you pay your fees and receive your course schedule. After so many months or years, you are given a certificate representing your accomplishments. At that point, you're on your way to the real job force because you are qualified to handle your trade.

These are the same steps you take to get over a relationship. First, you have to make up your mind that you want to enroll in the school of pain and graduate with a certificate of freedom. If you aren't serious about it, you won't get your degree. You might have to move, but there's nothing wrong with going to school outside of your state. Do whatever it takes!

After enrolling, you'll listen to previous graduates telling you that some days are harder than others and that some lessons don't take that long to finish. You will also discover that there are nights you spend worrying and scratching your head for hours trying to figure out the day's lesson.

Another characteristic of this school of pain is that sometimes there are surprise tests. They come in the form of you running into your ex when you least expect it, causing you to run around like a chicken with its head cut off. Sometimes the ex is with his or her new—and younger—love, sipping coffee together in a small café. You might fail the first surprise test, but have faith because that test will appear again, and you'll surely pass because you already know what's on it.

We must face the fact that the person is not with us any longer. The longer you stay out of school, the harder it will be for you to learn the lesson. Attacking the problem head-on. The Bible tells us that we are to be either hot or cold and for our *no*'s to be *no* and our *yes*'s to be *yes*. *Lukewarm* or *maybe* should not exist. "Maybe," always keep us wondering and indecisive.

This is why we have lots of problems today. We straddle the fence. Either he's going to be fully with you or he's not. Thinking in terms of "Oh, well [he or she] came home tonight, but maybe they won't tomorrow night" will only drive you crazy.

Enrolling in this school of pain and having Jesus as the teacher will make the lessons easier. If you stay in class, you're likely to become the class valedictorian; it's when you start playing hooky that you should expect the unexpected: dropping out and trying to register all over again. For God is still a God of second chances.

When we live our lives, we do not have the world's trouble on our agendas. Usually it's a bunch of wants and desires. We're looking for good things to come through our front doors, but trouble creeps through the back door. All of the money in the world cannot heal a broken heart; it takes time and the right medicine, such as the love of God to be poured in the wound.

If you don't want any help, don't enroll in school, and make sure you don't ask God to help you. You can leave your application beside the rest of the tombstones. I'd rather be alone and working for the Lord than to be with someone who is preventing me to get to Him!

COUNT IT ALL JOY

Can you imagine trying to count it all joy when frustration, temptation, aggravation, lust, and many other things tempt us? It is by our faith that we have to believe that we can overcome the problem. God has not forgotten us.

> My brethren *count it all joy* when ye fall into various trials, knowing that the testing of your faith produces patience, but let patience have its perfect work, that you may be perfect and complete, lacking nothing. If any of you lacks wisdom, let him ask of God, who gives to all liberally and without reproach, and it will be given to him. Let him ask in faith, with no doubting, for he who doubts is like a wave of the sea driven and tossed by the wind. (James 1: 2-6)

It will take time and faith. Think about it: You didn't become a teenager or adult overnight; it took time! You acquired the wisdom that you have today over a period of time, and you are *still* learning.

You will get to the point where you will want nothing but what God has for you. In the midst of your patience through this problem, you will still count it all joy, laughing away saying, "Is this the best the Devil can do." Which amounts to nothing when it's in God's hands.

God knows all of us. As he told Jeremiah in Jeremiah 1:5-Before I formed you in the womb I knew you; before you were born I sanctified you; I ordained you a prophet to the nations.

If we ask for wisdom He will give it to us—but it all has to be by faith. We fall into all types of temptations and make plenty of mistakes. Take, for instance, a woman who goes to bed with a man she doesn't love. She not only doesn't love him, but she doesn't enjoy the sex—above all, she gets pregnant and the man denies that the child is his.

At this point, she is like a dog standing in between two fire hydrants, not knowing which hydrant to pee on to relieve herself. Instead of asking God to forgive her and help her make a decision, she decides she wants vengeance. She throws bricks at his car, makes harassing phone calls, throws sticks through his windows, sends a letter requesting child support, and anything else she can think of. She never does get the man; she only gets a bad reputation. Now she has to suffer for nine months waiting for the constant reminder of him, plus puts herself in danger.

> Beloved, do not avenge yourselves, but rather give place to wrath: for it is written, Vengeance is mine; I will repay, says the Lord. Therefore if your enemy is hungry, feed him; if he is thirsty, give him a drink: for in so doing you will heap coals of fire on his head. Do not overcome by evil, but overcome evil with good. (Rom. 12:19)

Think of all the woman has done because this man didn't want to stick around. She's equally at fault for sleeping with him and then trying to destroy his life. They both need to take part in forgiveness. Will she reap what she has sown for breaking windows and throwing bricks?

She could have just counted it all joy, not because of the mistake and sin but because she still had enough breath in her body to ask God for forgiveness and strength to raise a child who may become a great icon to the world.

I once heard a story about a woman fighting with another woman over a man that wasn't either of theirs to begin with because he was married to someone else. Evidently he was cheating on his girlfriend on the side, while his wife was at home.

If you want to go good and crazy fall in love with a married person. Rest assured you'd have many lonely sleepless nights and many cancelled dates. You may be getting the best part of the sex but you'll never get the full enjoyment and you will **always** be second. It's like two dogs in the streets, and one is in front leading. Always remember that the second dogs view never changes because he is always looking at the other dog's butt.

In some cases the one who's married will try to control the single person's life he or she is seeing on the side. If the single person would get caught with someone, surely the married person would be highly upset! If he or she leaves their spouse for you, what do you think they'll eventually do to you, unless converted in the mind? As strange as it may sound there are couples who are into free love such as wife and husband swapping. Also for some cultures it is a natural thing to have two and three wives. It's hard for me to handle one. It's almost like a pastor who pastors' two churches. Somebody is not going to get as much attention.

Not to pick on one particular sin because we all have guilt somewhere. Our bible lets us know there is only one perfect person, which is Jesus Christ. Can you imagine the following cases of fornication?

1. A heterosexual committing adultery
   (Ex. 20:14) You shall not commit adultery
2. A homosexual/lesbian relationship
   (Lev.18:22) You shall not lie with a male as with a woman. It is an abomination.
3. A single person with lust in their heart

(Matt.5:28) I say to you that whoever looks
at a woman to lust for her has already committed
adultery with her in his heart
4. A married bisexual man or woman (all three)
   a.   lust in their heart
   b.   adultery
   c.   homosexuality

5. Two Christians falling into sin constantly having
sex. In this case the man decides to see someone
else in his weakness. The woman he has left, in
her rage tells him that he's going to hell for what
he is now doing. Why was the hell story
different when the two of them were together?

This is to let us know there are things going on in our
minds all the time regardless of how puffed up we may become. We are all jacked up. Can you imagine what would go
on in a males mind if he sees the true woman of his dreams
walking down the street the day after he had gotten married?
There are many different sins and it doesn't matter. We all have
something going on. This is the reason we shouldn't judge each
other, although we do. We'd rather judge the person than pray
for them. A straight girl asked a man why was he gay and he
said he didn't know because that's how he has always been. The
gay man asked her why was she straight and she said she didn't
know that how she has always been.
   **1John 1:8 reads: If we say we have no sin, we deceive our-
selves and the truth is not in us.** If we confess our sins, He is
faithful and just to forgive us our sins and to cleanse us from
all unrighteousness. **If we say that we have not sinned, we make
Him a liar,** and His word is not in us.

This is straight across the board regardless of your denomination. By the way I heard there's over 20,000 different denominations. Can you imagine every one being right? There is a generation that is pure in its own eyes, yet it is not washed from its filthiness (Prov. 30:12). Every way of a man is right in his own eyes, but the Lord weighs the hearts (Prov.21:2)

Understanding that particular scriptures lets me know that we need to ask for forgiveness everyday. We have enough battles in our minds that will almost drive us crazy. Can you imagine us doing everything that crosses our mind? God forbid.

As human beings, we can get ourselves into more crap than ever seemed imaginable, but it is the mercy of God that gets us out and forgives us for all our sins, whether great or small. There was an old saying that went: "All sin was once fun." Better yet, "How do you measure poison?" In other words whether small or large doses it is still poison.

The real enjoyment of counting it all joy is when the sin is so tempting but we don't do it. Instead, we laugh and say, "It was close, but thank God I made it." As you know we win some and we lose some and all we can do is try to be a better person. Not making excuses for sin, however we were born in it. It's like making Kool-Aid and now trying to get the cherry flavor out of the water. It would take a miracle to change the cherry colored water into clear. God is a God of miracles. Another scenario of this would be: Now take that same glass of cherry Kool-Aid and setting it under the water faucet. Now turning on the water allowing it to finish filling up the glass. You will notice that the clear water is beginning to push out the cherry color representing sin. Eventually the glass will be full of clear water representing Christ. I guess this would be a good time to say, "My cup runs over, surely goodness and mercy shall follow me (Ps.23:5).

In other words the more clear water we get the healthier we become, same as the word of God. The reason some people are extremely wild is because there is no guilt or conviction.

RELATIONSHIPS ARE NOT FOR EVERYONE

"The Lord God said, It is not good that man should be alone; I will make him a helper comparable to him" (Gen. 2:18). This is very true, but it doesn't necessarily mean that you have to marry a helper.

Woman was made from man, and she is to help man under divine instruction from the almighty God. As you know, when you can't get a man to do something, there's always a woman that is willing to help. Look at our churches today; most are filled with women who are helping, but some are hindering God's program at the same time. Very few men are standing up to women in the rightful manner. Many men allow them to go ahead and do what they please just to keep the arguments down. As once said, the wheel with the squeakiest noise gets the oil.

Unfortunately, since women's lib and women's desire to be equal as men there have been lots of problems (ask Satan, Isa. 14:12)—not only because of women's desire to be in everything and to know everything but also because of men not standing up for what they should. Of course, if the majority rules and there are more women around than men, what do you think is going to happen?

It reminds me of situations at private military schools for men when women after going through a bunch of changes, are able to wiggle their way in there. What men don't understand is that if a woman could initiate it, she would see to it that men would have menstrual cycles and have babies. When will men ever stand up?

When it comes to frustrations, ask Adam about it when

107

Eve began to feel differently about the fruit. Our frustrations today are because of the fall in the garden. Man listening to woman. God told Adam first not to eat of a particular tree (Gen.2:16). The serpent deceived Eve (Gen.3:1-5). So Adam and Eve were punished because Adam listened to Eve (Gen.3: 17). Adam sinned and Eve was deceived and they both were hard headed like we are all today. As much as a woman fusses, she really doesn't want a weak man.

A woman that rules a man really doesn't want a husband; she desires a slave. Because of our society and its way of thinking, it is very rewarding to be a woman. She can rule her husband like a man, and she can demand many things from our government system—from child support and alimony to being company presidents—where men dread to go. After making wrong decisions and being dominant, she can conveniently fall back into the weaker and meek role as a woman. Today I laugh when I hear the statement; "A man shouldn't hit a woman." Where does self-defense come in and have you seen some of these women hit? They are like professional boxers. Stand there if you wish.

As the scripture reads: "Husbands likewise, dwell with them with understanding, giving honor to the wife, as **to the weaker** vessel, and as being heirs together of the grace of life; that your prayers may not be hindered" (I Pet. 3:7). Hey, men: If you don't want your prayers hindered, help her out, but remember that it doesn't mean she has the right to continuously stir up problems because she is considered weaker, and in some cases purposely.

Now let's speak on the institution of marriage. "Therefore a man shall leave his father and his mother, and be joined to his wife: and they shall become one flesh" (Gen. 2:24). They are to become as one, and hopefully God has put them together.

Wives, submit to your **own** husbands, as to the Lord. "For the husband is the head of the wife, as Christ is the head of the church: and He is the Savior of the body" (Eph. 5:22). If a husband isn't following Christ, you have double trouble if the wife isn't either. Today 50% of marriages end in divorce.

If each spouse has his or her own selfish motives, it only leads to frustration. The husband winds up asking, "God, why did you make a woman if all she does is gets on my nerves?" The wife winds up saying, "God, you should have made woman first—and left it like that."

There are a greater number of women in our population; therefore, there are more women seeking relationships than there are men. As the scripture reads: "In that day seven women shall take hold of one man, saying, We will eat our own food, and wear our own apparel: only let us be called by your name, to take away our reproach" (Isa. 4:1). Meaning, the ratio of women to men will be 7 to1. It almost sounds like the man could be a pimp.

Where before the man would seek the woman, now the woman would be seeking the man. The woman would be bound to support herself and her man, leaving him without expenses. The only reason she'd have for marrying him would be for the label of *wife*, taking away the shame of being a single woman.

Today many women, in their weakness, are even taking care of men who have no desire to work. Other men are off at war, or involvement in homosexuality, or some are sitting in a jail cell for murder of other men or crimes. Their scarcity will only become greater. Can you see why seven to one now?

Relationships are not for everyone, and being able to abstain from sex is a gift from God. Because of the smallness of people's unlearned minds, some think that a person who isn't sexually active is either weird or gay. **Our Bible says not everyone can accept this teaching, but only those to whom it has**

been given. "For there are eunuchs who were born thus from their mother's womb, (they were born that way); and there are eunuchs who were made eunuchs by men; and there are eunuchs who have made themselves eunuchs for the kingdom of heaven's sake (renounced marriage). He who is able to accept it, let him accept it" (Matt. 19:11).

Some are born without sexual desires or the need for a relationship. Some eunuchs were made by man, in which the man was castrated (had his testicles removed) and had no sexual desire; the kings would make them overseers of their harems. There are others who, because of free will and the kingdom of heaven, have chosen abstinence. Nuns and priests know much of this. As we've come to find out today through weaknesses that there have been some Nuns who have aborted babies as well as priest accused of sexual acts. Can you understand Matthew 26: 41?—Watch and pray, lest **YOU** enter into temptation. The spirit indeed is willing, but the flesh is weak.

In the Bible, Paul refers to abstinence as follows: "For I wish that all men were even as I myself, **but each one has his own gift from God,** one in this manner, and another in that. I say to the unmarried and to the widows, it is good for them if they remain even as I. If they cannot exercise self-control, let them marry; for it is better to marry than to burn." (I Cor. 7: 7). This particular burn is burning with passion and feeling as though you need to have sex. "The can't help its."

Paul knew that when you are married, there are obligations to the spouse. He also knew that because of sex, the responsibility of children inevitably follows. When you are single, you may do the work of the ministry freely. Those that are married and also in the ministry sometimes have a dual task, which at times can be quite challenging and may at times hinder the anointing of God on the individual who is going to do the will of God. An argument or great disagreement can take the focus off the actual mission for the day.

I've told people that marriage is like living with your parents but you have only added the free will of having sex. You have to respect one another. Your spouse needs to know where you're going and most definitely where have you been.

I heard a doctor say once that when counseling engaged couples, he would ask each of them to give him three reasons for getting a divorce. After each gave him a response, he would tell them that they were not ready for marriage because there shouldn't be a reason for divorce if you love one another.

Relationships are great for those who want them and who are doing so according to God's will. When a relationship is not ordained by God, however, there will be great disappointments—you can mark my words. Living in frustration every day can be quite depressing, causing low self-esteem, high blood pressure, and openings for other diseases due to the lack of joy in the relationship. You would be surprise of all the diseases in the medical books that are related to stress. When a bad relationship leads to a household that stays in a consistent uproar, it is better for someone to move.

It doesn't make any sense to live in hell and also die and go to hell for those that believe in it. The reason I put that clause there is because everyone does not believe in hell. As once said, "What if you died and found out there wasn't a heaven or hell?" On the other hand, what if you died and found out there is? It's just like insurance, better safe than sorry. The word assurance and insurance work together. In other words be confident (assurance) that you are covered (insurance).

We must constantly seek the strength and the will God has for us in our lives. Various partners who are not in tune with God can one day possibly lead to a "fatal attraction." There are many scriptures in the book of Corinthians pertaining to marriage.

Personally, living alone gives me great freedom and peace. In some cases where I lived with others, I became a hermit in my room because I just so happen to love privacy. I create when I'm alone. Although I have many creative gifts and have met lots of people I am basically a loner. How long this will go on I do not know.

After being alone for a while and achieving a few goals we tend to get sentimental. All of a sudden there's no one to share these achievements with and the next thing we know we're in a relationship. After a while we seem to be pressured to stay in it. It is hard for some people to live with anyone. For some couples, it might be a good idea to go ahead and get married but live in separate houses. Some couples even have their own bedrooms and of course it depends on the "real" reason. In other words, everyone needs his or her own space. Do whatever works!

Search your heart and make sure your decision is working for you and you feel comfortable in it. Enough problems will come unaware. Why live in one that you know for sure? After all you're going to be with yourself the rest of your life. *Romans 14: 5 reads: One person esteems one day above another; another esteems every day alike. Let each be fully convinced in his own mind.*

Just a reminder: Separate rooms may work for a while. After which there is a longing for love and affection from somewhere. Only to lie in your bed and fantasize of being with someone else. What's so ironic you may have once fantasized of being with the person you now desire to leave. In some cases the separate room arrangements are fine while on the other hand someone may be wishing for the other to die to get the freedom they really want. How sad! Believe me some people have been immune to a negative relationship and holding out to the end. Whether there is love or not only thinking of the benefits. Your partner have a good idea if you're cheating and everything else. Once again as quoted in Jeremiah 17:9- The heart is deceitful above all things and desperately wicked, who can know it?

Furthermore we don't know everything. For we know in part and we prophesy in part. When that which is perfect has come, then that which is in part will be done away (1Cor. 13: 9). As you do not know what is the way of the wind or how the bones grow in the womb of her who is with child. So you do not know the works of God who makes everything (Eccl.11:5).

Take the bible for instance with its many unanswered events. Only God knows. We just add our little beliefs to what we think may have occurred during that time.

Our spirit tells us not to marry, but we ignore the feelings of doubt. For some reason we know something doesn't feel right and we just can't put our fingers on it. So we go on and do what society dictates to us. You can go to all of the psychic readers you want and waste your God-given money, but the true answer sits in your heart.

In my first marriage, a little doubt lingered all along before the marriage—all the way up to the date. The morning after the ceremony, I asked the Lord, "What in the world have I done?" I stayed married about two years still wondering how I got into such a mess. When you have to wonder, try not doing it so late. Just to refresh your mind, realize that marriage and dating are two different sports, and the rules of the game are different. A client of mine said the funniest thing to me one day. He told me to fix him up real nice because he was going to a funeral that day. I asked, "Who passed?" He smiled and said, "No one, a buddy of mine is getting married."

We must be extra careful in seeking relationships just for holiday seasons. Man has pressured many into thinking that they need to be with someone during this commercial yet lonely time. Loneliness during the holidays is only temporary, but all too often it leads to severe depression, suicide, unwanted pregnancy, and disease. Let's not get stuck with someone for the wrong reason. It will only cost you later on down the road. We're to deck the halls not wreck the halls.

Having a good helpmate, male or female is great whether married or unmarried. Helpmates for sex are different than helpmates for friendship.

Remember what God has joined together, not you!

UNCOVER THE LAUGHS

There is a lot of joy and laughter deep inside of you that needs to be uncovered. That peace and happiness has been covered with blankets of sadness, sheets of lies, quilts of frustration, and comforters of jealousy, surrounded by skirts of fear. Getting out of that bed of depression and stepping into a steam bath of joy is the only thing you should be looking forward to.

There is nothing like an uncomfortable mattress. You toss and turn because it is either too lumpy, too hard, or springs are sticking out everywhere. Who can sleep in peace on something like that? In the same token the mattress can be of good quality but the human mind is restless and at war.

Your spirit's frustration and unhappiness became so cold that you piled on more layers for warmth. Negativity wanted you to die out and smother you, but for some strange reason, you stuck your little head from underneath the covers and smelt a little fresh air. It was the refreshing scent of God drawing you.

In every woman there is still a little girl, and in every man there is still a little boy; therefore, when there's a big problem, we must run home to Daddy! God is our Father, and He wants us to talk to Him.

Have you ever wanted to tell someone something that had been aggravating and burdening your mind for months and sometimes years? Once you got it out, regardless of the consequences, didn't you feel better? That's how we have to talk to God. Although He already knows, still tell Him what's really bothering you. As Matthew 6:8-15 reads—When you pray, do not use vain repetitions as the heathen do. For they think that they will be heard for their many words. Therefore do not be like them. **For your Father knows the things you have need of before you ask Him**. In this manner, therefore, pray:

> Our Father which art heaven
> Hallowed be thy name
> Thy kingdom come
> Thy will be done in earth
> as it is in heaven
> Give us this day our daily bread
> And forgive us our debts
> As we forgive our debtors
> And lead us not into temptation
> But deliver us from the evil
> For thine is the kingdom and the power
> and the glory forever. Amen

For if you forgive men their trespasses, your heavenly Father will also forgive you. If you do not forgive men their trespasses, neither will your Father forgive your trespasses.

Open your mouth. Don't let the Devil make you think you are going crazy because you are talking to yourself. Have faith! My definition of faith is believing in the positive regardless of the initial outcome—because God knows your heart!

If a blind person has enough faith to walk down the street with a cane, why can't we have faith with our eyes wide open? The blind person has to have enough faith in what he can't see and what he believes in his heart.

Uncover the laughs. Take the distressful quilts off one at a time. "A merry heart does good like medicine: but a broken spirit dries the bones" (Prov. 17:22). You need to restore your joy.

Attend fun and exciting events; watch funny movies. Something is bound to make you laugh again. Don't dry up and crack.

If you think you don't have anyone now, wait until friends don't want to be around you because you start bringing the whole party down. It's not that they don't understand; it's just not their time yet to be depressed.

Do you remember hearing the story about the "lucky" lady who was going to marry a millionaire? He paid for everything, but the only problem was that he never showed up to the wedding. Guess what? She had the last dance because she went on with the reception and danced and had a wonderful time.

Now that's turning a bad situation into a good one. He hurt her, but at least she started getting over the pain early in the game.

Another good true story I heard was about a famous man who was very ill. He had been in the hospital for many months. As he began to read his Bible, he came across the scripture "A merry heart does good like a medicine" (Prov.17: 22).

He thought about it and then told his wife to go and get all of the Laurel and Hardy movies she could find. (In case you're too young to remember, Laurel and Hardy were comedians who made millions of TV audiences laugh.) The man and his wife watched the movies every day, all day. To the doctors' amazement, the man walked out of the hospital a short time later as a new man full of joy.

You see, laughter strengthens you and keeps you strong. Have you ever noticed that older adults who always have a lot of children around them have so much spunk and joy? Being around a sad person every day is not healthy for anyone. It's just like a healthy person deciding to go to the store and buying a pack of diseases so he can get sick.

Imagine that you were depressed and met someone who

was more depressed than you. You probably would say, "Let me get my butt out of here; she's making me worse." You have to go where you can get strength and help. You never know where it will be coming from or when it will arrive; it's just like the wind.

Who's to say that this joy won't come from a church you visit? It may or may not, but you need to hear the word of God and the stories of faith through everyday people like yourself. Don't think that everyone singing and smiling and jumping up and down for joy in church hasn't had similar problems.

Remember that your hurts and pains are only temporary. They are training you to help someone else along the way, someone that has given up hope. Once you are an expert on pain, you will share your stories—and hopefully this book, too—so that others will know that the end of something is better than the beginning. "We are all bought with a price and we have to pay up every now and then and respect the real owner of us all" (I Cor. 6:20).

Uncover the laughs and seek joy. Protect your heart; when it gets damaged, take it to Dr. Jesus. He's a good healer, and he knows whom to refer you to—because he still has a good staff on board that works twenty-four hours a day.

NOW THAT I'M FREE, WHY AM I SO PICKY?

Thank God you can see the light. Once free, it didn't seem to be as bad as you thought, did it? The Devil is a mean artist, and he can paint a devastating picture.

You have gone through each day praying and hoping to overcome the pain, filling your extra time with new ideas and new people—in Christ I hope. One day that pain just eased away. It was so smooth that you found yourself looking for it but couldn't get it back. You worked at getting it away and didn't realize you lost it.

God will lead you to the point that you have to let go of everything and seek Him. "Seek first the kingdom of God, and His righteousness; and all these things shall be added unto you" (Matt. 6:33).

When you go seeking you will find out many things that you didn't know existed. Above all you will find out yourself of how little you really know.

Perhaps you sought someone out first, even though deep in your heart you knew it was wrong. Now you are crying, frustrated, and wondering how to get out of it. Hopefully you're asking for forgiveness and asking God to help you. Remember: He has always made a way of escape. When it comes to our spirit, we must abide.

"No temptation has overtaken you except such as is common to man: but God is faithful, who will not allow you to be tempted beyond what you are able; but with the temptation will also make the way of escape, that you may be able to bear it" (1

Cor. 10:13). Look! If God says you can bear, then bear it! The only way you can heal a wound is to treat it, then watch for the results.

The problem we have is seeking Him first because the Devil has put so many material and physical obstacles in front of us. God is spiritual. "It seems hard to seek ye first when God has given you two eyes."

You have one eye on God and the other eye on the prowl. Until you bring both eyes together, you will have a hard time regardless of the relationship or task. **Seek Him with your whole heart.** God will not have it any other way. We can kick against the pricks all day long and just end up being a prick-kicker with no testimony and still finding life hard. Like Jesus told Saul in Acts 9:5; "I am Jesus, whom you are persecuting, It is hard for you to kick against the pricks (goads)."

Unless we give up all in our spirit to seek God, we will be constantly going around in circles. I twirled my Hula Hoop® around so many times that I almost turned into a solid ball. If a person told me to pray, I prayed; if they said seek the Holy Ghost, I sought after it; if they said take a three-day fast, I fasted.

I had to make up my mind and seek all I could. I wanted to know who this God character that kept pulling at me was. Once I found Him, I wanted to seek more. You can never get it all. If He'd put all of His glory in us, we would burst. Did you hear me say, once I found Him? As though He was lost, knowing I was the one that was lost. Therefore with loving kindness I have drawn you (Jer.31: 3). God is drawing us all the time. We have to give it up and think of God spiritually.

Assuredly I say to you, there is no one who has left house or brothers or sisters or father or mother or wife or children or lands for My sake and the gospels, who shall not receive a hundred fold now in this time—houses, and brothers and sisters and mothers and children and lands with persecutions; and in the age to come eternal life. (Mark 10:29)

If you do not put your trust or faith in all of these material things and seek God, He will give you more sisters and brothers in Christ. You thought you were losing one person, but in actuality you are gaining many more whose spirits will unite with yours, but with *persecutions*. Unfortunately persecutions come along. In other words you may have a gorgeous new car, but every now and then you'll still get a flat tire.

People will always have something to say whether you're doing good or bad; the Devil has to slip his doubt in there somewhere or he will lose his job. To God be the glory, because one day the Devil will be fired! Persecutions will cease.

Now that you are free to see things differently, have you noticed that your eyes are more open? You've become very picky about whom you associate with and what they talk about. You have that right, and you have the right to make your request known unto God. Months ago you couldn't breathe, but today you are sucking in all of the air; you can make sincere decisions now. If someone fails you, or vice versa, you will handle things differently; you won't drag out pointless pain for years.

Regardless if you're wealthy or not, people can read in between relationships to see if there is any real fire there. The rich can cover up pain materialistically, but it's hidden in the heart. It similar to putting a nail in a piece of wood; if you pull the nail out, you cover the hole with many layers of paint, but you still know the hole is there. The poor don't have the benefit of the rich to cover up feelings, so they are exposed all day long with a very sad countenance. A psychiatrist was asked would he rather counsel the rich or the poor. His reply was the rich, because they know that money isn't the answer to everything.

It is only through the power of God that there is hope. Now that you're free, ask God to pick what or who is best for you—even if it's just a good friend! Paul said that he wished all were like him, free, so that they could do the work of the ministry, not worry about what time they should get home! (Smile)

We all have "issues." However with each new printing the reading gets better and better. Stop going to the newsroom and picking up old back issues of loneliness and misery. Every now and then the new issue may get a little torn before delivery, but thank God its not full of the old crap.

Now that you're free don't be so picky that you miss your new blessing. If you're seeking to reap perfection in others you just might have to sow it in yourself first!

As I was once told from a dear friend:

"It's a rough life out there, but somebody has to live it."

ABOUT THE AUTHOR

Stewart Marshall Gulley is a man whose life has been surrounded by all types of people. The joy and concern he has for humanity has astounded many with his talents and gifts, which he recognizes as extensions of God's hands. After having been in countless relationships and married twice, through biblical principles he is willing to share with others how to overcome distressed minds and broken hearts. Although he feels man has tampered with the bible he goes by his gut feelings and so should you.

Mr. Gulley recognizes that we all go through some type of emotional turmoil after the loss of a long-term or short-term relationship—some go through as much pain for the loss of a pet.

Mr. Gulley's guest appearances have opened the minds of many, as he uses the word of God through his everyday analogies. After living in five different states, attending nineteen different schools; being a member of nine different denominations; holding numerous jobs; marrying and divorcing twice, he has discovered that everyone somewhere goes through some type of emotional strain—regardless of the job, location, or position in life. Which ranges from the pastor to the prostitute, God has allowed us to all feel the pain of loss.

Mr. Gulley believes that we can only express the joy of overcoming a wrongful relationship by actually going through it with the help of God. "Yea thou I walk through the valley of the shadow of death, not around it.

As often need to be thought of is, the end of a thing is better than the beginning" (Eccles. 7:8).

OTHER BOOKS
(Soon to be realased)
BY STEWART MARSHALL GULLEY

- Hear No Evil, See No Evil, Speak No Evil:
  A Guide for Biological Parents, Grandparents and
  Stepparents
- Baby, You Make Me Smile
  (Twenty-five short stories with lesson plans)
- Everyday Life
  (Over 200 Poems)
- If You Thought Columbine Was Something You
  Haven't Seen Anything Yet
- I Love God, But Church Makes Me Sick
  (Why Churches Are Weak) (It takes more than
  preaching)
- Adam, Eve Is Out to Get You
  (Young men being fooled by women)

www.ingramcontent.com/pod-product-compliance
Lightning Source LLC
Chambersburg PA
CBHW071128250626
47159CB00006B/2173